Where ⌐

Marti⌐

Copyright © M⌐

Front cover design by Anne Cakebread – Copyright 2022

Dedication

For me

About the author

Born in Liverpool in 1978, Martin Cakebread lives in London. He has lived all over the world from an early age, in Africa, Asia, the Middle East and Europe. This is his first work of fiction. Martin is a former Director at UK Defence & Security Think Tank – *UKNDA*.

Try to imagine.....two young people, deeply into each other. 'Need I say more?' said Jack. Fast forward five years to February 2012 when 'all hell broke loose'. Heart pounding through his chest, 'all I could think of was my love' said Jack. 'I didn't know if an attack on me was imminent or not, I knew nothing.' 'All I knew was that I was scared out of my life.' If the Russians and Chinese were 'professionals' there should be no reason to be afraid thought Jack. But this was different. Try to imagine the movie *'The man who knew too much'* (Not that I've seen it) he thought. But this movie title should give some indication as to where this is going. Jack and Nikki had not long been engaged. Deep in the back of his mind, Jack feared being part of the Defence & Security organisation *UKDO*. Albeit a voluntary organisation, it consisted of politicians, former and current. Leading military figures, former and current. Along with ordinary members of the public. He came into that category. After years of watching members of the UK Armed Forces being killed in Iraq and Afghanistan, Jack decided to do something, essentially to try to, well, help. How you might ask? He joined a Defence and Security think tank. *UKDO* wasn't especially well known to the public. But rather in defence and security circles, it was considered to be potentially, highly influential when it first formed and in subsequent years. The officials of the organisation were all under surveillance. Not just by UK Intelligence. But intelligence agencies from across the world. The US, Russia, China. You name it, even the Saudis had their informants. *UKDO* was where Jack met Mike Scott. They hit it off from the word go. In fact, it was Mike Scott who nominated Jack to become a Director at *UKDO*. The significance? Mike was about to become a Member of Parliament (MP) in the UK. He was a former Colonel in the British Army. A former member of MI1. He had served in both Northern Ireland and Bosnia. His reputation was second to none. He was good friends with former UK Prime Minister John Minors. He was also a mason. Jack on the other hand was just a well-informed, low level political player. Having spent the previous decade campaigning on local issues, he had a kind of 'break' when he became a strategy consultant for a review into government spending in 2005 during the general election. He was also lead writer for conservativefuture.com at the time, in addition to being a constituency chairman, he tried repeatedly to become an MP. But unfortunately, he had no backers. No money and wasn't a mason. Jack had never held any elected roles, he just had political interests. Namely, UK Defence, Security and Foreign Affairs. Ultimately, Jack wanted to be a political analyst or advisor. 'Boy how that was a waste of time' he said some years later. It didn't stop his primary problem. He was now under surveillance and didn't actually know. He had his suspicions from the start of joining *UKDO*. He didn't get excited and think he was suddenly a spy. Quite the contrary. He kept his feet on the ground and tried to come up with practical solutions to help UK Defence. But time and again, he being the news buff, started finding his so-called ideas in the UK media? He couldn't believe it at first, he told no one. Then suddenly thought, 'what if I'm under surveillance?' So rather than panic, although he admits, he was scared in the back of his mind, he started throwing out obscure ideas. Like suggesting the Hollywood actor well known for the phrase 'I'll be back' to visit the UK and quote, 'terminate the deficit' (check it out online). To his surprise and horror, the day said actor visited *Downing Street*, the UK Prime Minister stood outside the front door and said 'he's going to terminate the deficit' coincidence or something worse? It was Jack's suspicion that he was now under surveillance. Crazy you might think, impossible even? But Jack couldn't work out why there was an unmarked police car outside the front door of his flat? It had its police badge on the dashboard. Jack thought it just coincidence and carried on with his day job at a US tech start up near Kings Cross. 'You had to be there' he said. 'It is impossible to explain' he went on. 'Only the people watching and there had to be people watching know the truth and that can only be a very small number of senior people around the world.' He went on 'the only way I can explain this is to put pen to paper and hope that someone would believe my story.'

'We've all been there. In love that is. It is a difficult thing to lose especially when you're married let alone explain'. 'I sacrificed love, my love to try and save me, my family, you name it. It was the most painful thing I've ever done. It literally tore me apart', said Jack. 'Funny thing is, as I write this', said Jack, 'I can't remember for the life of me what love was truly like at the time. I just knew I was truly happy'. This isn't a love story by the way. This is about surviving what was an absolute nightmare in real life. 'I doubt many would believe what happened, but I cheekily hope one day, someone will make a movie out of it.' For a six-week period Jack didn't sleep one bit. 'And when I say a bit, I mean a bit'. His stomach seized up in knots like never before. Fear was the word. It gripped him in a way, that it almost paralysed him. Driven purely by adrenaline. It was physically exhausting. The lack of sleep. The intense indirect pressure. The job, the marriage, life. All flashing before Jack's eyes. I mean put yourself in Jack's shoes. 'You're being followed by what you believe were Russian and Chinese agents, practically on every street corner'. How? Why? How could Jack know? He was observant. He was one of those kinds of people, who paid attention to everything, and 'I mean everything'. It was even more intense when things started going wrong or should we say 'off'. Unlike actual spies, Jack had no training, no skills for this situation he found himself in. It was the death of the Libyan Oil Minister, found face down in a lake in Switzerland (check it out online) that did it for him. Along with a whole host of suspicious 'deaths' like the woman stabbed a single time found dead in a garage lock up in London, newspapers reported at the time she was thought to be a spy, involved with the Libyan conflict? Lots of multiple deaths, deaths that Jack paid attention to in the news. He then started looking through the articles on other deaths, like that of the 'spy in the bag' a year or more earlier and the British man in China who was allegedly killed for helping a political figure. (Check it out online). But reality was it felt like a coordinated assault on anyone who had anything to do with the Libyan operation between 2010-12. 'Terrifying isn't the word. It was horrific'. Said Jack, Why? Jack had provided all the ideas to get the Libyan leader killed. Indirectly via email at least. Jack thought 'shit'. Anyone who actually reads or read the transcripts of what I said during the Libyan operation would know that I was the one who came up with the idea to start 'electronic jamming' let alone 'cut off the head of the snake'. To Russia and China, Jack was guilty. Guilty as the politicians who used his ideas. You see, Jack's emails to colleagues at *UKDO*, in private, were all under surveillance. Jack said again 'Anyone who looks back at the records would assume I may as well have been running the operation'. He went on 'I was so scared, because unlike actual spies, political advisors, or politicians, I was 'outside the ring of protection'. 'You see, I was a volunteer, a civilian, a nobody'. Then why the hell did the Russians and Chinese turn up and harass Jack so badly even to this day in 2022? He still doesn't know, but suspects it was Libya, his friendship with Mike, and everything he said online. 'Be very careful what you write online, people are watching,' said Jack. Jack was convinced he was a 'person of interest' and on a possible 'hit list' for Russians and Chinese, he could never know, but indeed he was. 'Thank god I never went to *Downing Street* with Mike' he thought. A year earlier Mike had wanted to take Jack to *Downing Street* to meet the Prime Minister at the time, David Norris. 'Now I think about it, I wondered why when I went to visit Mike on more than one occasion an American 'tourist' literally stopped to ask directions just before he went into to Portcullis House'. Coincidence, or just a tourist? It was the CIA. Jack had no idea, but again thought back at that moment, how convenient it was that when he was on his way to see Mike, an American would stop him literally at the front door? Coincidence it had to be. Why think this twice? Because Jack was like that. 'Where was UK Intel?' thought Jack. Breathing heavily, as he approached his apartment block. He looked up to see the unmarked police car with two officers inside, a man and a woman. Jack started crying, thinking that his time was up. He feared an assassin was waiting for him in his flat. He got in the main front door and cried a bit more. Tried to gather himself. Walked slowly up the stairs to his flat. He couldn't work out why he was thinking an assassin was waiting for him; he just had this god awful fear running through his body. He approached the front door and went in thinking this was his last few moments on the planet, gripped by fear, not bravado, he had no energy, no will to fight. He just wanted to run away. But wanted to get home first before his wife to be just in case. To his almighty relief, no one was in the flat. He broke down in tears again. Not very manly now he looks back, but it was the honest truth. He looked out the window, down to the unmarked police car. He looked out the back window only to see a marked police car, yes, marked. He thought 'shit, what the hell is going on here?!'.

That night he made sure everything was locked; he got a screw driver and put it under his mattress, kept his base ball bat nearby and put a hanger on the front door handle and lay awake all night, listening out for anything suspicious. To his horror, around 4am he heard what must have been two cars stop quickly and men jump out shouting at someone telling them to stop. It was the police, hard stopping would be assassins sent to kill Jack and his wife to be. Jack heard the whole thing. The next day he got up having not slept a wink. Tried to eat, whilst nearly passing out only moments earlier. He remembers the moment well because the news was on the TV and it was all about the Prime Minister's young three year old daughter who got plastic stuck up her nose and had to go to hospital (check it out online). Jack was livid. He was furious with whoever had been giving his ideas to politicians, if not top politicians in the UK and possibly US. He thought if he wanted to 'survive' this episode, he had to pay attention to every detail and wrote emails to himself that very day describing everything he had seen and experienced. (He could hardly start telling people, they'd think he was crazy, besides he hoped his email were under surveillance too). Still no contact from UK Intelligence. He didn't know what more to do. After changing his route to work and back, he was scared. Returning home that night, it was the same again, police outside and later than night as he lay in bed listening, a car screeched to a halt outside men jumping out and someone was being taken away. It was scaring the hell out of Jack. He had to work, hold down a relationship, you name it, live life. It was impossible. So the following day he went running to try and 'reset' himself, only to recognise a woman who walked right by him outside his flat. It was the Russian agent who killed the British agent, the man in the bag as reported in the news, 'check it out online' said Jack. 'In fact, if you look back at many of the events described above, check out online and you will find much I have said to be true'. All Jack knew was every time he went out there in London, there was a Chinese agent walking past him, eyeballing him. It was so obvious, the intimidation that was. The Russians were harder to spot, the real spies wore grey macs. But 'we will come on to that' he said. 'I kept thinking about the movie *Octopussy*, the opening scene where *009* is being hunted through East Berlin'. 'Hunted'. What a word thought Jack. 'I'm being hunted' he said to himself. Nowhere to run, 'who could I tell?' he thought? The only difference between this and a movie was that Jack wasn't a spy; he was now no longer a Director at *UKDO* but a civilian. The President of the United States, a President Jones was being fed daily intelligence reports from Jack, via the CIA, 'I mean imagine, all you had to do was mention President Jones in an email to a colleague and hey presto, it was reported back to the President first hand via his team.' Jack had no idea but took a punt on this. I mean think of it, actual government decisions being made indirectly by Jack. In hindsight, Jack should have gone to his friend in Parliament, Mike and should have said, he was being followed. Instead, he took all the pressure by himself and it nearly destroyed him. He stupidly thought, 'perhaps if I go to the doctor and claim depression, the Chinese and Russians will leave me alone? Never do that' said Jack. Jack now had a medical history that most would run a mile from, resisting seeing a psychiatrist for years, he feared being locked up. Jack wasn't stupid, he knew if he started coming out with crazy conspiracies about Chinese and Russians harassing and following him. He could be in trouble. Indeed, some years later he would be briefly detained. But that is another story.

So instead, back in 2012, Jack thought, how best can I get out of this mess? He decided to write emails to himself, apologising for his indirect role in providing ideas to help in the overthrow of the Libyan leader. He also took out multiple life insurance policies. Yes life insurance policies. You see, should he die under suspicious circumstances there would have to be an investigation. He hoped should the worst happen; someone would work it out. He never had to use the life insurance thankfully. China knew it was Jack's ideas that were in play, but they had no proof he worked for anyone let alone knew officially he was under surveillance. The CIA who had Jack under surveillance couldn't work out what had 'spooked' him, excuse the phrase. Why was Jack so scared, what was it? The British and Americans didn't even bother to look into the situation; they just thought he was having a 'breakdown'. He was indeed, thanks to the almighty cock up by UK and US officials. Jack emailed himself addressing the mail to '*Don Cesare*' he had a suspicion who he was talking to – a former Italian Prime Minister and famous political figure, Silvio Di Marco. Two years later UK intelligence would be caught directly spying on Italian phones; emails etc (check it out online). Meanwhile, Jack prayed for 'extraction' to anywhere, (Bermuda ideally) by anyone who would help. It never came. Jack was exhausted. One night he heard a scream outside his flat. It was a woman. The same he had seen the night before walk past him. The assassin. She had been tasered by the UK authorities and swept off to an interrogation unit somewhere in the west country. Jack decided that the best thing to do was to move from Barnes in South West London, to further down the road to Richmond. Jack had lost his job. He was booted out after losing focus and unable to perform. He had no idea what was next, other than, he had lost his job two weeks before he was supposed to be married. One evening sitting in a pub in Richmond, he turned and saw a suspected Russian agent in a grey mac leant against the bar. Jack saw him and decided to call his bluff by shouting out loud 'Mike Scott is a great man' Jack turned and looked at the agent, who had the look of horror on his face and quickly ran out of the pub. The crowd went quiet albeit briefly, then everyone went back to their drinks as if nothing had even happened. The agent was never seen again by Jack. The next day, Jack saw two goons, this time in their light tan macs and backpacks on, glaring at him as he got into his car.

Jack assumed they were both Russian, sent to intimidate him. Jack now clearly on edge had to try and hold it together but deep down feared he couldn't. He had to his own admission made a fatal error. He went to the doctor to complain of 'depression'. He realised immediately the error in his ways, he could easily be sectioned or locked up if he started coming out with anything 'off the wall', he would later tell his psychiatrist, he believed quote that 'Vladimir Pushkin' was out to get him. Another bad move. Jack went for months terrified that he would be locked up all along trying to reassure his wife to be everything was 'fine' when clearly it wasn't. Anyhow he kept waiting for a 'signal' or even some kind of basic contact from UK SIS; but there was nothing. One morning as he stepped out of his flat in Richmond and an RAF Hercules flew over him, he assumed it could be a signal and then remembered he lived right under the flight path and it was impossible to know. 'What could it mean?' he thought. It went round in his head for ages. He naturally assumed wrong. Night after night he lay awake in bed trying to work out what to do and wondered if his friend Mike would indeed 'rescue' him? A car he thought has to come by road and then airlift out by helicopter from Richmond Park. Jack at this stage was completely worn out. He wasn't thinking straight one bit. His train of thought was badly affected. Jack panicked and on a call to his dad, the first thing he said was 'ambush!' in the hope that anyone listening would know what he meant. He kept hoping the 'good guys' were listening in, but by this stage it was just the Chinese and Russians. Meanwhile, President Jones asked the head of the CIA what was going on with 'Osama Bin Ahmed' code name for Jack Cakebread (check it out online). The President ordered his CIA officials to stop listening in and cut him loose. They merely watched as Jack was degraded month after month. No one had the guts to help Jack. The Russians and Chinese closed in. Jack had no choice but to push ahead with his wedding on the 14th of July 2012. Fearing the worst. The week of his wedding, it was reported on *UK News* that a French assassin was on the loose in England. Jack assumed after him. (Check out online). Jack pressed ahead with his wedding plans, taking every moment to plan how he would be the first to intercept any would be assassin at his wedding. Jack would use the knife on the table on the pen he purposely carried in his pocket. It was a marriage that unfortunately would only last six months. But that wasn't the fun bit, Jack and Nikki jetted off to Venice, Italy for honeymoon. He feared the worst yet again that this time the Mafia would be waiting for him. Jack and Nikki flew business from Heathrow to Venice, had a car from the airport all of one hundred metres to his private motor launch where it took them to the front door of one of the most prestigious hotels in Venice. Low and behold the mafia were waiting for him at the airport. They 'cruised' past him numerous times wearing their aviator sunglasses. Jack had to hold it together. As he sat on the launch to hotel he thought for a brief moment, he was the reason why the Libyan leader was dead, indirectly at least. But fear and reality gripped him once more. It was blisteringly hot. Jack wanted a break, to go for a day without seeing any Chinese or Russians. No chance. In the four days in Venice, he walked the streets, and the Chinese and Russians made their presence known.

Jack then drove to Sirmione on the southern tip of Lake Garda to a quaint but slightly dated hotel for the remainder of his honeymoon. On day two he looked out of his window only to see a Chinese couple taking photographs of his bedroom window and hotel with a large telephoto zoom lens camera. He quickly hid behind the curtains. That night he had a really vivid dream about Vladimir Pushkin, Russian President, where he saw him vividly. Jack didn't want to be tracked so he did everything he could to convince his now wife to leave her phone behind so they couldn't be tracked. They subsequently wandered the small peninsula that was Sirmione. The holiday and marriage was a strain. Jack just couldn't get the possibility of being killed out of his head, all along trying to 'protect' his new wife. Upon returning to the UK, Russian and Chinese agents continued to follow and harass him. Some months later, Jack standing on the steps of Chelsea townhall where his sister had just got married, Jack saw two Chinese men in suits photographing him again with large telephoto zoom lens cameras and the entire wedding party was oblivious except Jack. Yes, everyone oblivious to it apart from Jack. Jack wanted to scream. Just another example of what was happening to him. Incidentally, he thought by going to the doctor to 'pretend' he was quote 'depressed' would in turn ease the pressure on him. It only made matters worse. All along pretending there was something wrong with him. Only some ten years later would he be locked up for being high and arguing with his then new girlfriend. The police would detain him, but that is another story. The problem was that the Russians and Chinese were very astute when it came to espionage and conflict. They had followed and revisited everything he had written to colleagues at *UKDO* and found Jack 'guilty' for the death of the Libyan leader. Jack thought 'how can they hold me guilty, I have merely aired opinions in private?!' What Jack didn't know was that Russia and China had been using psyops against him. They were amazed he had made it this far. The Chinese have actually developed psychological and telepathic spy techniques. It is messed up. (Check out online). They had used these techniques on Jack and continue to this day. Western intelligence are aware of these capabilities, however, dispute their effectiveness. Jack confirmed it worked on him. 'I will spare you the detail and focus on what I saw and know happened' he said. 'It was truly terrifying. Try to imagine MK Ultra via satellite or drone, let alone whatever the Chinese where up to'. A year after his divorce, he went to Whitehall, in Westminster, London. In the vain hope of seeing his old friend Colonel Mike. By remarkable chance, he saw him. Jack stood opposite Downing Street holding a map of London, pretending to be lost. Then from the rear of Old Scotland Yard emerged, Mike with three staffers, who Jack didn't recognise. Mike also saw Jack and recognised him. Both walked towards each other. Before Mike could say anything, Jack knew they were probably being watched, so Jack wanted to help Mike, he thought what can I say? Knowing he'd probably never see Mike again. (He did but that was some years later). Jack quickly said 'I am a Liberal Democrat now' to which Mike bluntly said 'piss off' turned and walked away. It was surreal. But Mike had been under massive pressure to cover up the fact that the UK government had had Jack under surveillance. The Americans in particular wanted answers as to what had gone on, but only at as an aside. Jack knew, Mike would be found 'guilty by association' – 'guilty of what, I will never know' said Jack. 'If anything I should have been rewarded. I lost all confidence in Prime Minister David Norris after that'. Many years later it was reported by UK media that current and former UK SIS agents were being harassed and followed by Chinese agents *en masse* – (check it out online). Jack felt vindicated, just wished someone, anyone would get in touch with him and hire him to work for them. He now wanted to be a spy. Up until that point he wanted nothing to do with the whole world of espionage. To him, he was a political advisor, not a spy. Now having seen first-hand the scale of operations worldwide, he felt like having a go. So applied to join MI6 some years later in 2018. Much to Jack's amusement he was rejected. Probably wrong school, not a mason, wrong university, and wrong demographic, go figure. Try to imagine Jack found jobs here and there and just couldn't hold them down. Finding his predicament unbelievable having been put through hell. Fast forward to August 2022 Jack was working again but still being followed by Chinese agents everywhere he went. Jack's Twitter account clearly stated that he was a former Director at *UKDO* and he deliberately pinned a tweet which showed 'Cakebread' was the official US code name for Osama Bin Ahmed (check it out online).

He said 'think of the movie *From Russia with Love*, where Sean Connery arrives in Istanbul, Turkey. He turns to his driver and asks if it is customary to be followed, only to receive a response, oh yes.' Jack was followed everywhere; he suspected the Chinese and Russians must eventually believe Jack would become an SIS Officer or perhaps someone would make contact? Either way Jack felt 'alive' with his newfound Chinese connection. Every time he saw the Chinese, he loved it. Ironic that he had gone from fear of death to loving life. But in the back of his mind he knew it was still serious.

Anyhow the significance of Twitter was that Jack regularly Tweeted to the UK Prime Minister and other political figures in the hope that they would ask who he was, internally at least. Come August 2022, they did just that. A senior advisor saw his pinned tweet about his code name, and they investigated who 'Cakebread' really was. 'A no one' said that SIS official. Keen to dismiss any possible significance, you see Whitehall politicians including civil servants have egos and the one thing they hate is praising anyone. Had they only known what Jack had been through and how keenly to this day he was under surveillance by China and Russia. If only. But actually Cakebread's file said 'top secret, restricted eyes only'. The SIS Official didn't want the politicians to know what had actually happened to Cakebread, so they made up a story. Anyhow, the month of August in 2022 was highly significant, (check it out online) Prince John took money, a million pounds cash, from the Osama Bin Ahmed family. 'I would have had him shot; the Prince that is' said an anonymous SIS source. 'To think UK Troops were fighting and dying, and that Royal dickhead, was taking money from our enemies.' Jack agreed. It was some ten years later, Jack still waiting to be contacted by SIS. Sitting in deepest Bavaria, in the southernmost tip of Germany, just under Hitler's 'Eagles Nest' amusing thought Jack, so he decided to tell his story. Meanwhile as monotonous as it seemed, Chinese and Russian agents continued to follow Jack on his travels, first on the plane from Heathrow to Munich, then at various other intervals. He wished almost that they'd talk to him. This was something that eventually happened, but that was for another time. Jack saw himself as an 'ideas man' plain and simple. It was why the Americans and British had had him under surveillance in the first place, because they were so utterly clueless, they needed multiple sources and Jack was one.

President Jones now retired, found himself advising the current President Joe Sullivan who was even older than him. President Jones exact words were: 'put Osama Bin Ahmed' back under surveillance. You see it was Jack's idea to create the new city in the Saudi desert called Neom, it was taken off him by who, he didn't know, but it was something he had suggested previously. But that was all small fry really. Russia had invaded Ukraine and well everyone was waiting to see what China would do *vis-a-vis* Taiwan. Jack decided to keep out of both. He didn't want to be 'blamed' again. This time, rather, offering 'suggestions' on how Ukraine could defeat Russia. But actually he believed, the serving Ukraine President was actually 'harming' Ukraine via a prolonged conflict he couldn't win. Jack believed the Ukraine President should go into exile in neutral Switzerland extracted by the USA. Fighting would only prolong the destruction of a beautiful nation, that was so vital to Europe and the Worlds food security. Jack wasn't 'pro Russian' *per se*, rather, looked at the situation practically. His experience watching the conflicts of Iraq, Afghanistan, Libya, Syria. He realised the importance of knowing 'when you're defeated'. 'Cut off the head of the snake' Jack infamously said regarding the Libyan leader. And it was. Jack played dumb many years later and actually searched for, found and emailed a UK Libya expert to ask why it was that the former Libyan leader wasn't extracted and sent into exile? The reply he received didn't inspire him and indicated that the said expert didn't know what she was talking about. The former Libyan leader didn't go into exile because Jack made sure he didn't, indirectly at least. No doubt he regretted that, quite significantly as it happens. Jack had also hoped by contacting this expert it would flash up on the UK Intelligence radar and they would remember him. Alas, it wasn't the case. Jack had long predicted the likelihood of simultaneous attacks and we saw that take place in India and France respectively. Jack always thought he was under surveillance from the USA especially after visiting the US Embassy for an event in London back in early 2000s. As an aside and in private, he recalled vividly discussing with someone the idea of a simultaneous attack on a capital city being virtually undefendable. Not long after, Mumbai happened. Then Paris.

'That's the thing about politicians and I say this sincerely having wasted way too much time following politics and being involved at a low level, politicians will sell out anyone or anything to get what they want.' Jack was sold out said SIS Agent X: 'It goes on to this day. Jack has been treated very badly by both Russia and China, but ultimately the US are to blame for putting his views in front of their political leaders.' Jack in 2022 was weak. His body a wreck. He felt like an old man. But maintains seeing the Chinese around 'makes him feel alive'. 'Osama is back' he laughed to himself. He wished he never went to the doctor in the first place, he wished he had never caused his family so much grief. Jack's advice was simple to people reading this: 'never go to the doctor if you're depressed'. Jack had grown up across the world from a young age and actually never understood why SIS hadn't approached him prior? One thing was for sure, Jack cheekily some might say, wanted his 'cut' from Libya. The money disappeared so quickly it was unbelievable and as for the oil and gas revenue, he didn't see a penny until one day he was hired by the Bank of China as Chief Marketing Officer. But that indeed is another story. Joking aside, Jack couldn't work out why he was still being followed all these years later? Did China and Russia genuinely believe he was responsible for Libya? Or was it something more sinister? Most people wouldn't even notice if they were under surveillance. Jack on the other hand had a fair idea. Jack even asked the Chinese in an email to himself to make him an SIS Officer posted to Hong Kong, but no joy..yet. He sometimes wondered about his former friend Mike in Parliament. How he was doing? Jack would regularly comment on various websites directly mentioning Mike as a top MP in the belief someone political 'was watching'. You see, being a little political operative, he knew who the major political players were and that political parties used what is known as social media monitoring technology. Whereby, they could monitor online what was said about an MP or all MPs (check it out online). Jack knew this. And played to it to shape Britain indirectly, all from his keyboard.

Jack found himself regularly picking up tails, this time a guy who looked like 'odd job' in his smart BMW 5 series. But it was the guy some weeks earlier on his way back to his flat, when he looked up into his rear-view mirror he looked in the eye of this Chinese mini driver. Clearly unsettling the driver who started playing with the camera on his dashboard and some strange antenna, so Jack smiled in the mirror then sped off. This was a common occurrence for Jack, he just couldn't work out it was all meant to signify? He just suspected that should conflict breakout over Taiwan he could easily become a target of the Chinese. At least so he thought? The more Jack looked at the situation, the more he couldn't understand the so called 'animosity' between West and East. It felt unnatural and almost forced. Perhaps a declining power in the United States was now intent on stirring up trouble across the globe so as to draw the Chinese into conflict? And in turn cost them trillions of dollars or renminbi just as Iraq and Afghanistan had effectively 'broken' the US financially speaking. What were the Americans thinking thought Jack? 'I mean the 9/11 terrorists were Saudi!' said Jack, yet, Iraq was attacked and 'regime change' sought? What a futile act that cost the lives of countless good military men, let alone the destruction of life as ordinary Iraqis knew it. Now we have the vacuum of US withdrawal from both countries, whilst all along interfering in Syria and goodness knows what they're doing with Libya? Libya could have turned into a beacon of hope for Arab nations. But it too was destroyed by warring factions, intent on exploiting the nation. Jack didn't sign up for that. When he indirectly helped Prime Minister David Norris and President Jones, it was done because he believed in freedom and democracy, not exploiting the wealth of a sovereign nation. Libya has since declined and despite some tediously slow progress, has not achieved anything by way of stability or normality. If the US actually had more of a presence there, perhaps they could have rebooted the economy and society. Speaking of booting, it was Jack who reminded his would be surveyors of 'Operation Boot' whereby Iran was subverted covertly to install the Shah of Iran in the 1960/70s if not earlier. 'I fear the US, who, with the greatest of respect, are so insular, decided to embark on a journey of destruction. Not even knowing why in the end, but the Libyan leader should still be alive. No doubt about it.' Jack would have loved to be an analyst for SIS along with a senior political advisor to the Westminster elite. Alas, that would come, but not before he turned fifty...in a twist, Mike found himself still struggling with the trauma of war. Jack noticed this, when he knew Mike, he knew Mike had difficulty coping with the horrors of war that he has witnessed throughout his career. But none worse than what he saw in Bosnia. Becoming a Member of Parliament was a mega achievement for Mike. He never thought he'd make it, but becoming an MP meant that he was now accountable to the people. Taking up his seat in the House of Commons, he had a lot of contempt for the masses of MPs who were truly awful, creepy, greasy pole climbing types. Mike didn't know if he could influence the new Prime Minister David Norris but he knew he would try. Mike probably more than Jack or at least on the same level got the big picture. That namely the UK was cutting its Armed Forces at a critical juncture in its existence. It was absolutely vital to spend more on defence and security, yet, these vital departments would be cut and badly. To Mike it was unbelievable. He had made it to Parliament only to find it impossible to convince the new PM of the need to spend more on Defence. Over time Mike gave up. Jack never did. Jack thought that the best way to approach this was a long-term project, bit by bit, as he always said 'little drops of water make a mighty ocean'. Jack would continue for years, not for his own benefit, but the ultimate benefit of the nation. He found it entertaining to watch how politicians took his ideas from the internet and employed them. Jack knew the UK was on the cusp of spending more on Defence and Security. The year was 2022 and there was a leadership contest on in the Conservative Party to become the next leader and ultimately new Prime Minister. The leading candidate had indicated that defence spending would increase to three percent of GDP. Jack wanted five percent. So he continued to Tweet and Blog to that effect, knowing that it was just a question of time. Moreover, thanks to Russia and China ironically and their new geopolitical positions on Ukraine and Taiwan, they had in turn spurred the UK to review its defence and security posture. Something that Jack had called for a decade earlier. How the UK was so far behind was unbelievable, but you see, the problem was modern day western politicians didn't plan for much except getting re-elected. That was a major problem. No planning for energy, food or military security. No strategic interests. All seat of the pants stuff. Careless and irresponsible you could argue. Anyhow, Jack watched as his country fell down the GDP rankings, debt increased and the economy shrank. It was a disaster. All started by the 'global financial crisis' back in 2008. Did you know Jack was the first to coin that phrase online? Boy the Conservatives made a huge mistake not hiring Jack as an advisor. Could Britain survive? Living beyond its means with ridiculous spending on guaranteed, yes, guaranteed civil service pensions which had a liability of over two trillion pounds. Jack long advocated their demise, but no one listened. But these over generous gold-plated pensions would eventually be stopped just like they were in Greece during their financial meltdown. And yes the year was 2022. Britain had run out of money. It was a repeat of 2008. Actually caused by the Consumer Credit Act 2005 which the then Labour government had introduced as a means of making it way easier for people to borrow, risky lending as some would call it. It led to the collapse of the UK banking system which still some fourteen years later the UK hadn't recovered from. Yet to Jack's amazement the former CEO of Bank of Edinburgh got away, Scott free for his part in the collapse of the country's biggest international bank. Jack had his moments where thought like the Russians and he thought said CEO should have been found face down in a river somewhere. But then Jack had his moments like anyone..and the list was long..Jack believed firmly that Treason should be made an official punishment including white collar workers and in particular politicians. But hey, this was a democracy. No doubt the majority of the UK public actually wanted execution for murder to be made legal, let alone anything else. But Mike now a politician found himself on TV quite a lot at first. He was regularly interviewed and when the British soldier was beheaded in London he went on air saying that he would have shot the terrorists dead. Britain had lost its way. Whereby foreigners could come and go with impunity, or rather, prosecute their vile agenda with rape, murder and other terrorist related activities without punishment for fear of 'offending' certain demographics. Jack regularly watched the news as countless non-British types rampaged with impunity. Jack had had enough and wanted to change the way the UK was governed. Mike too regularly shook his head in despair. Knowing that his political bosses had little backbone or will to make Britain Great once more. Instead, mismanaged decline seemed to be the order of the day. Mike found himself regularly in the House of Commons bar having a skin full. In fact it was the very next day that would change his life. It was a beautiful sunny morning…

A beautiful, crisp Monday morning you might say, in Westminster, London and it had just begun with the usual buzz about the place. Politicians and staff arriving for morning committee meetings and the like, with a spring in his step MP Mike Scott had just finished drinking a cup of tea in his office. Talking about the weekend's campaigning with his staff. He found himself looking out the window as he put on his tie, tying the knot, he turned to the mirror in the corner of his office and fixed himself up right. Putting his collar down, he then turned to his desk chair and reached for his jacket. Calmly, he picked it up, putting it on and again turning to the mirror. On the lapel, a small clip on badge glimmered in the light. It was a badge from the Parachute Regiment. You see, Mike Scott, or Colonel Mike Scott was a former commanding officer of the First Battalion, often referred to as being part of the Special Reconnaissance Regiment (SRR). For Mike or 'Magic Mike' as he was known by some, it was an immense honour to have served as an officer in the Regiment. 'The Paras' as they are known are a fierce some bunch. Renowned for being the first into a fight. For Mike though, his fighting days were over, or so he thought. Now he was in his early sixties, a Member of Parliament for the first time. He had always had an interest in politics; after all, most of the operations and missions he was sent on were politically motivated one way or another. He was good friends with Ted Maguire a former MI6 agent and former leader of the Liberal Democrats. He also got on well with former Prime Minister John Minors of the Conservative Party, who sent him on his first major command as UN Commander in Bosnia. Suddenly, the door slammed, and Mike twitched ever so slightly. His eyes shifted to the corner of his head and for a moment, he had a flash back to the horrors of Bosnia back in the 1990s where he witnessed first-hand countless atrocities and murders. Let alone the numerous times he was in contact with the enemy. Killing around twelve enemy soldiers during the time he was there, which was a lot considering he was supposed to be keeping the peace. He also lost countless numbers of his own men, including his driver, who had his head blown off by a sniper whilst out on patrol. Mike was an immensely popular figure not just in the Army, but also, in the House of Commons and Westminster as a whole. He commanded authority and respect from a huge range of people, often finding himself drinking in the Commons bar with some of the most unlikely of characters from the Labour Party. You see, Mike was a Tory at heart and represented the Conservative Party as Member of Parliament for the constituency of Kingston-Upon-Thames of all places. As Mike, recomposed himself, he stood up one last time before he headed out of his office down into Portcullis house for breakfast with his staff. On the way there, bumping into the Secretary of State for Work and Pensions, Esther McCarthy. A top woman, with great charisma and strength, and former TV presenter. 'Morning' he said, with a cheeky grin on his face. 'Morning' back Esther replied. They both stopped for a moment to talk shop in private. Mike telling his staff to order him the usual and get a table in the dining area. Mike was on his way to meet Jack Cakebread who was waiting eagerly in the Portcullis House lobby. 'Is it true?' he said to Esther McCarthy with an air of concern. 'How can the PM seriously be thinking of cutting back our Army, when the threat assessment levels are through the roof' Mike exclaimed. 'The Cabinet was told late last night of both the PM and Chancellor's desire to quote, streamline, Defence further.' Mike's face began to turn red with anger, 'well that's bloody ridiculous if you ask me, I mean how on earth are we supposed to defend ourselves? We will be the laughing stock of the military community.' Esther shook her head and said 'we tried to stop them, you would be surprised how many Cabinet members openly criticised the plans and actually wanted a vote on the matter, but the PM refused flatly.' Mike put his hands in his pockets and rummaged for some loose change, 'you see, even John Minors knew the importance of the Army despite *Options for Change*, it feels like the current PM is clueless, unable to see the wood from the trees. And all along today we had Prime Ministers Question time, you watch, those bastard's opposite will have found out and will rub it in all day long' he said It was late 2016, David Norris had just been replaced by gangly new leader and new Prime Minister Rebecca Matthews. 'I know' said Esther. 'Well, as US Army Colonel Hal Moore often said, there is always one more thing you can do' and with that Mike strode off to the lift and down out to the courtyard and into Portcullis House lobby to meet and greet Cakebread. 'Good to see you' said Cakebread. 'Yes, good to see you too' remarked Mike. Let's head over to the cafeteria. 'Bacon sandwich good for you boss?' said Ed Thomas, Mike's political advisor and senior member of his team. 'You what? Yes sure' Mike quipped. Still preoccupied with his conversation with Esther. Mike spoke 'very posh' English according to some and his command of the language was powerful. Hence why he was such a good public speaker.

Meanwhile, whilst sitting down with his team and the variety of other MPs and their staff also munching away, totally oblivious to the world and chatting with Cakebread about *UKDO* Mike had forgotten Jack's quip about being a quote Liberal Democrat (which was total BS). Jack was introduced to various MPs as they walked past. You see, Mike having been part of MI1 knew all about surveillance. When he became and MP and a secret defence advisor to the new Prime Minister, he got told that members of UKDO were all under surveillance. Hence why he wanted to see Cakebread, not to tell him, but he had heard Cakebread had been indirectly making a big impact with his ideas and views. He turned to Cakebread and said 'I don't think they'll move on defence.' When suddenly outside the main building at Portcullis House, a jeep came screeching round the corner over Westminster bridge, hitting the brakes hard and coming to an abrupt stop in the parking bay out front. Four men jumped out of the vehicle and ran towards the revolving doors of Portcullis House. Heavily armed, with AK47s, RPGs, a backpack full of loaded magazines, grenades, and oh don't forget the C4 and remote detonators they were about to lob on the main doors and detonate. They quickly and carefully placed the C4 on the glass doors. Suddenly, a huge explosion ripped through the lobby of Portcullis House as they detonated the explosives. This left a huge crater in the ground, the receptionist and security staff were blown up completely. Totally taken unawares. Bodies laying on the floor and body parts strewn over a wide blast area. The four terrorists who had hidden behind their jeep, rushed in, past the mangled security scanners and came across another security screen which was bullet proof. They placed more C4 on the door and screens, ran back out, and detonated again. As they did, Mike immediately knew something wasn't right hearing the initial blast, he ordered his staff and Cakebread to return up to his office immediately in the Old Scotland Yard building next door, (which served as offices for MPs and their staff). In fact, there was panic and pandemonium in the canteen. People running everywhere and smoke and fires erupting in the main lobby. Mike knew there was nothing he could do, he was unarmed and getting on a bit. So he fled upstairs with his staff and barricaded the office doors. Once inside calling up the Prime Minister's Chief of Staff, a slender, goofy individual known as Dan Washington. Not liked by Mike as they had regularly clashed. Mike urgently shouting down the phone that Portcullis House had just been hit and was under attack. Even Washington who was outside talking to journalists at Downing Street had heard the loud blast. Smoke by this time was billowing up through the main atrium of Portcullis House and outside the main door.

By this time, the four terrorists had entered Portcullis House, jumping through the flames that had engulfed the main entrance. Two with their AK47s, one with an RPG launcher and one with a PKM, they sprayed the courtyard and cafeteria with bullets. Killing at least fifty people, a number of MPs and their staff were killed instantly. Grenades were thrown, causing mass casualties in the kitchen and dining area. One terrorist fired his RPG into the crowd. The wounded lay on the floor, crying out for help and one by one the terrorists executed at point blank range each and every one of them. Suddenly shots came in, an unmarked police officer opened fire, missing the terrorists, only to have an entire magazine emptied into him at about ten metres away. He bounced in the air as the bullets hit him and then thud, hit the floor hard with blood everywhere. Portcullis house was now on fire and the sprinklers were only partially working. The two explosions had caused a lot of structural damaged to the building and part of the front was about to collapse at what used to be the main entrance. To anyone caught up in this melee shouts were for help and police, yet there were none. This wasn't normal as Westminster had practiced a terror attack and police response. But what the people in Portcullis didn't know was that this wasn't an isolated attack. Quite the contrary. This was part of a simultaneous attack by multiple teams of terrorists on Westminster itself. One at Portcullis House, one at the main entrance of Westminster where cars drive in, one at Black Rod's entrance and one at the side entrance of the House of Commons main security entrance. These attacks were devastating, taking out the police on guard who were totally outgunned and outnumbered. The terrorists using overwhelming fire power including vehicle mounted PKMs, blew away all the police guarding Westminster. The firefights didn't last long. Although the sound of sirens was in the distance, the second team of terrorists had blocked the road and were using cars and trucks as barricades. It was chaos. Try to imagine Parliament Square blocked by traffic and four jeeps, one at each corner of the square opening fire on anything that moved. It was a brutal sight. Bodies everywhere, vehicles exploding as bullets penetrated petrol tanks, buses on fire. That very day, hundreds of tourists were in the Square sightseeing and visiting Westminster Abbey. RPGs fired across Parliament Square at the House of Commons smashing in to the ancient structure and exploding. Each jeep had a driver, a gunner mounted on the rear, and three other passengers with their AK47s pointing out the windows firing away. As the four speeding Police Armed Response Vehicles (ARVs) arrived from Lambeth bridge direction, a hail of bullets and RPG rockets met them. The terrorists had studied TV footage of the routes taken by police when responding to the last terror attack on Westminster. It was all too easy. Unlike the Americans whose police were all armed, the UK only had a limited number of armed police – eight armed officers in four vehicles to be precise that morning in the vicinity. It was frightfully easy for the terrorists to take out the response teams. They fanned out across Parliament Square taking up defensive positions at all four corners and randomly opened fire on any passing vehicles or pedestrians. Cars were on fire, dead bodies of tourists lay in the street. By now from twenty four terrorists, the death toll was well over two hundred people in the first twenty minutes. The incredible power of automatic weapons and rockets, that the British Security Services had dreaded since the Mumbai attacks, was on display. A police helicopter and *UK News* helicopter circled overhead. Filming live TV, the ensuing devastation on civilians down below.

Meanwhile, across London, five other terrorist teams comprising of ten men each, had unleashed their attacks on London Bridge station, Waterloo station, Victoria station, Paddington station and Liverpool Street station to deadly effect. This was clearly turning out to be a very well co-ordinated, planned and resourced attack. With rush hour thankfully just over, the casualties were lower, but still hundreds had been gunned down as they went about their business. The police were totally overwhelmed, in fact in many instances, the police where nowhere to be seen. With their armed response vehicles totally outgunned and outnumbered, unarmed police units were ordered out to take cover. It was desperate. Fires began to burn out of control at countless office blocks as the terrorists dug in. This was a one way mission, the terrorists had suicide vests strapped to themselves loaded with ball bearings. Aside from being heavily armed, they were well trained on causing maximum damage in urban areas. Moreover, used secure radios to communicate with one another, knowing that the mobile networks would be switched off eventually by the police. Terrorists took aim at CCTV cameras and fired disabling them so that the Police watching from their command centre were partially blinded.

By the time the anti-terror hotline was buzzing at No.10 Downing Street and at the Met Police HQ. Police commissioner Janus was panicking, she didn't know what to do. She ordered all firearms officers to report for duty asap and immediately called for a situation report. What she learned terrified her. She leant to turn on the TV and *UK News* was broadcasting live across London, with reporters relatively close by to Westminster, Victoria and London Bridge. Commissioner Janus picked up the phone to the Prime Minister Rebecca Matthews and immediately said 'the situation is out of control Prime Minister, we have no armed police in the area and the terrorists have free reign'. The PM for a moment was short of breath, already accused by many of being out of her depth in a crisis, well, now this was the mother of all crises and she panicked. Dropping the phone, she scrambled to pick it up. Suddenly a bang on her office door, she jumped, her National Security Advisor Max Trentworth rushed in. 'Prime Minister, it is a simultaneous terrorist attack, a bit like that of Mumbai. We are totally outgunned and the police have reported mass casualties across multiple locations in central London. What shall we do?' he exclaimed. Nothing but silence ensued. The PM was in shock. The NSA got her to sit down and drink a glass of water. He then turned to the Chief of Defence Staff James Granville who smartly had rushed over to No.10 during the chaos from the MoD building in Whitehall and he issued orders immediately on his secure satellite phone. His *aide de camp* also got on the phone to the London commanders in the Army and put them on high alert, war footing. Live rounds and weapons were issued to all soldiers stationed in central London. The SAS and SBS were ordered to London from Hereford and the South West of England by helicopter, and SAS stationed at Regent's park, London, were summoned to a rally point at Piccadilly Circus. It had been a lucky moment as the SAS in Hereford had been undertaking a live firing exercise. Practicing with their brand new M249s from the manufacturer, their new M40A3 and M107 Sniper rifles, new Sig Sauer P226 Navy pistols, along with M40 grenade launchers and M4 machine guns. Meanwhile, ten Chinook helicopters were put on alert from RAF Odiham in Hampshire and they were fully fuelled and tasked with ferrying the various SAS and SBS men onto the roof tops of the MoD buildings in Whitehall and onto Horse Guards parade with their equipment. Apache gunships were ordered in as well from bases at RAF *Northolt* and AAC *Wattisham*. The problem was much of the Apache fleet was being repaired and only two were available, but the pilots were not on base. Nevertheless, the station commander ordered the helicopters be readied for tasking. Some thirty minutes later, the pilots had returned to base and were gearing up for departure. It would take another thirty minutes to reach Westminster and that applied to the Chinooks who had a two hour round trip. It would be some time before the Special Forces would arrive in Westminster. Plenty of time for rampant death and destruction. Finally, upon arrival in Westminster the Apache's immediately began to search for hostile targets. They had not received permission to open fire on the terrorists, so circled overhead. Hovering over Parliament Square, they radioed to HQ for permission to engage. They opened fire on the terrorist positions, taking out three with their chain guns. The other thirteen terrorists moved in to join their comrades in the House of Commons from Parliament Square, rushing the entrance. By this time the RAF were also ordered to secure the UK airspace and all flights were grounded over the UK. RAF Typhoon fast jets launched from RAF *Northolt* and *Conningsby* respectively. Approximately ten aircraft were eventually launched. Air to Air refuelling from RAF *Brize Norton* also set off and two RAF Sentry Early Warning aircraft were put on alert at RAF *Waddington*, one launched and headed to London. Meanwhile, the remainder of the terrorist teams now inside Westminster Parliament, House of Commons, rampaging and killing at will civil servants, political advisors, members of parliament – none were spared. Helicopters hovered and swirled overhead, all along were being filmed by live news TV channel *UK News*. Other news helicopters were ordered out of the area, prompting the head of *Global News*, Rupert Newsome, to call Prime Minister Matthews directly from New York and demand his news helicopters be granted permission to film live over London or she would lose his media empire's support during the next election. She promptly gave the order to allow the news helicopters to remain airborne much to the fury of CDS James Granville and other military types listening in on the radio.

General Granville, ordered a COBRA meeting and chaired it. As this was a War time situation, he took command with the Defence Secretary. Immediately a map of London was up on the screen and discussions were taking place of what to do to regain the city. With so many firefights taking place across multiple locations, a co-ordinated assault was needed but that would take quite some time. When the Mumbai attacks took place, it took more than three days before the Indian Army could control the situation. British Soldiers from their barracks in *Wellington Place, Hyde Park* and *Woolwich* were all being readied to move into the city and engage the enemy but this was nearly an hour after the first alert went out. David Gouk the Justice Secretary openly claimed that the human rights of the terrorists must be preserved. To which a unanimous response from the entire COBRA meeting was 'shut up!' and officially noted. It would take some forty eight hours before normality would return to the streets of London. The Defence Secretary ordered, armoured vehicles like the Mastiff and Ridgeback used in Afghanistan, to be deployed. The problem was, they were based far from London. No precautions had been made in advance, the Army only had jeeps and flat bed trucks. The call went out to get the armoured vehicles to London on the double but this too would take some six hours to mobilise. Meanwhile, the Army in London were trundling up major routes to surround, the various railway stations that were under siege. With the many of the approach roads of London now deserted and traffic being diverted away by police, this had become International news, across every radio and TV outlet alike. Live rolling cover was coming in and from the *ETV* studios on the river Thames; you could see plumes of smoke over large parts of London.

Mike Scott was itchy; he didn't like the idea of being locked in his office with the possibility of terrorists bursting in and killing him and his staff at point blank range. He had witnessed similar killings in Bosnia and the last thing he wanted was to go down without a fight. So he snuck out of his office, ordering his staff and Cakebread to remain until he returned. He went to the next office and again banged on the door, whispering for Esther McCarthy. She came to the door and he went in. 'What on earth is happening' she said, nervously shaking. 'An all out terrorist attack by the look of it. Mass casualties. You can hear the helos overhead and gunfire in the distance so this is far from over.' He said, 'But what are you going to do?' she replied. 'Wait here, I'm going to try to get to No.10 and see what's going on. If I make it, I will have a security detail come over here to escort everyone out. But for now the best thing is for everyone to stay put.' He said. 'Shouldn't that include you' she said, 'nope' was his reply. Mike managed to get to the ground floor of the old Scotland yard building, a building that had been converted into offices for MPs and their staff just next door to Portcullis House. He was lucky as the four terrorists had taken the escalator downstairs to go under the road through the tunnel to the House of Commons. The fires in Portcullis House on the other hand were now well and truly roaring, Mike peered round the corner and could see the flames and dead bodies laying about the place with pools of blood and broken glass and shrapnel everywhere, not to mention, bullet casings. He turned and went back out the back exit to a side street just opposite No.10. He managed to run across the road to No.10 where he was ordered to lay on the ground by police and Army who were at the gates. The gates which were now also barricaded with vehicles. A soldier approached him. 'Colonel Scott is that you?' he asked. 'Yes' Mike replied. 'Well get the bloody hell up and get in here' shouted the squaddie. Fortunately for Mike, many of the squaddies knew who he was, being a former Colonel and all. The main gates opened and Mike ran as fast as he could to the main door of No.10. Once inside he was ushered to the COBRA meeting room. Where he met and spoke with General Granville and the young Defence Secretary John Williamson. Mike immediately had an air of calm about him and that helped the other politicians compose themselves. 'Where is the PM' he asked. 'She had a panic attack' said General Granville. Mike looked at him with despair, rolling his eyes. 'Ok right, what's the plan?' he said. General Granville's *aide de camp*, then spoke up and gave a sit rep based on what they knew. Which was that 'Westminster had been totally overrun by possibly ten or twenty terrorists. That five main land railway stations were also under attack and that the military was on war footing and had already engaged the enemy via Apache gunship' the *aide de camp* went on, 'it is estimated at the moment that casualties run in to the hundreds, if not thousands, based on what we have seen.' Mike replied 'well, then we need to fight back and secure Westminster first of all, once done, we will then re-take the main land stations and mop up any resistance where we come across it.' The General then chipped in and said, 'the Special Forces numbering fifty are on the way to the MoD roof and horse guards awaiting instructions. Battalions from all barracks in the city are on war footing and waiting on the surrounding roads for orders to engage.'

With only three of the terrorists in Westminster dead, that left twenty one who were still roaming room to room in the House of Commons firing at anything and starting fires to force people out of hiding. The terrorists were carrying jerry cans full of petrol, they doused offices and hallways with petrol and lit fires with flares as they progressed throughout Parliament. Some twenty minutes later the ten Chinook helicopters were heard hovering overhead. Fast roping down off the rear of the five helicopters over the MoD building and the other five helicopters actually landing on Horse Guards parade one at a time. 'Go, Go, Go' was the announcement over the secure radio as the twenty five Special Forces closed in on the House of Commons from the MoD building. The other twenty five ran quietly along bird cage walk, then snuck past the Supreme Court, looped around Parliament Square, hugging Westminster

Abbey. The regular Army who were still waiting for the armour to arrive at bases, would eventually close in on Parliament Square from Victoria Street, Whitehall and Westminster Bridge and with their armoured vehicles would drive over the burning wrecks to secure a pre-determined perimeter blocking off Parliament Square from Whitehall and Bird Cage Walk. All along the Apache gunships provided cover from above, however, had to refuel intermittently. 'Area secure' reported a Captain in the Household cavalry standing on the square looking up at Big Ben, with its scaffolding on fire. 'We are going to need the fire brigade in pretty sharpish or the entire place is going to burn down' said an SAS Sergeant over the radio. General Granville ordered the fire brigade to rally points behind the regular army and at first that proved very challenging. Just like after the Manchester bombings, the fire brigade unions refused to order their personnel out and attend the fire. A huge argument broke out, in the end soldiers were sent to man the fire engines. Mike Scott went mental over the radio to the fire chief telling him to 'get off his fucking arse and get out there now'. 'We will deal with you later' said Mike.

Snipers took up positions on the top of Whitehall buildings. It was just a question of time before firefights would finally begin between the SAS and the terrorists, it was brutal. The SAS took out seven of them in quick succession, having the latest thermal imaging equipment and helicopter sights helped to give them the advantage and understand their precise movements and location. By now drones were flying overhead as well and fast jets buzzing the city. Door to door, room to room the SAS went one at a time – it took ages. 'This is taking forever' said an SAS trooper to his Sergeant. 'I know, get the hoses out and put out that fire!' the Sergeant said. Westminster was an old building and as a result the vast wood panelling that adorned much of it was alight. Bodies were everywhere, it was like an apocalyptic scene. The fires began to take hold and the SAS had to fall back. There were only fourteen more terrorists left. By this stage, Parliament square had been cleared by the Army once the order was given to move in. Burned out vehicles would eventually be moved to the sides of the roads but that would take forty-eight hours. Bodies would also be piled up neatly in a line on the pavement. But right now, literally two hundred soldiers had set up sandbag barricades at all corners of the square and bridge. Suddenly there was a huge crash as the front of Portcullis house collapsed. Two terrorists ran out into the street having run out of ammo, they wanted to conduct a martyrdom operation, but were shot dead by a group of SAS troopers. Now, only twelve left, the SAS had again returned inside the main building despite the fire and smoke. The SAS closed in on them thanks to the thermal cameras of the Apache helicopters. Bang, bang, double tap, three more terrorists were gunned down in the main entrance of the House of Commons. Automatic gunfire was heard through the House of Commons with terrorists spraying the Commons Chamber with bullets and petrol. Four took up defensive positions behind the Speaker's Chair and waited for the SAS to try to enter. As the SAS went in, the terrorists opened fire, killing one trooper and injuring a corporal in the legs. He crawled back only to be dragged back further by an SAS Sergeant Major. A major firefight was taking place and ten more SAS men entered the House of Commons lobby, taking up defensive positions and covering one another. The SBS however, had come up the Thames via four RIBs from Vauxhall bridge. They opted with grapple hooks to climb over the wall from the river and breach the Commons Chamber from the rear. But to their surprise they were met with a hail of bullets as four more terrorists in defensive positions opened fire killing two SBS men and injuring two more. The SBS Captain radioed in his situation and the Apache overhead saw two terrorists run out onto the terrace, opened fire killing them both instantly. Fires were now out of control. The SAS ordered to withdraw and the same with the SBS. The Chamber of the House of

Commons was set alight by the terrorists and those still alive, ran outside to the terrace where they would try to jump into the river Thames. Three swam across the river to St Thomas' Hospital and managed to commandeer a car and speed off westbound to *Vauxhall Cross*. Where they would attempt to breach MI6 Headquarters detonating their suicide vests at the main entrance. The Palace of Westminster was now eighty percent on fire. It was now too dangerous to enter. The British Army had now surrounded all of the Palace of Westminster and Portcullis House too. With the area now secure some five hours after this had initially begun, the soldiers managed to get the fire engines up close and connect to the main hydrants, getting some water onto the House of Commons. But it was too late in many areas, the fire had taken too much of a grip and the building partially collapsed also. Now Parliament Square was finally secure, General Granville and Mike Scott wanted to inspect for themselves first hand. They ordered the Old Scotland Yard building to be evacuated and a security detail dispatched to do so. With staff flooding out onto Whitehall and ushered towards Downing Street, there were hundreds of staffers running and crying. Granville and Scott surveyed first-hand the devastation and destruction of Westminster and they were both angry, accompanied by the Director of Special Forces and ten SAS men they stood by the Mandela statue to witness firsthand the devastation. Fortunately, years of training had helped them when they needed to be calm most. For this they would later both receive a commendation for bravery from the Queen. Along with the entire troop of Special Forces and a number of George Cross medals for squaddies too. But that would be for another day. Right now, there was still the problem of the five railway stations under attack on fire. Both Granville and Scott knew they were going to need more men. So they ordered a ten more battalions to central London, with another ten on standby on the outskirts of London awaiting instructions. This however, was a logistical nightmare. The British Army was not ready for such an attack and it took twenty four hours to muster all the battalions. Calls for the Prime Minister to address the nation were coming in loud and clear. There would be panic and the public would be scared. So Prime Minister flanked by Defence staff went on TV. They were partly there to 'g' her up a bit. She had overcome her panic attack and managed to give a reasonably calm assessment of what had gone on. Praising the military and telling people not to go near the main land railway stations until it was safe to do so. It was now three in the afternoon, it felt like an eternity since this first began around nine in the morning. The smouldering wreck of Westminster was akin to that of the terror attacks on the Twin Towers of 9/11. Caught on camera live when the roof finally collapsed, the flames were still burning from the mess and smoke billowed into the air, thick and dark. A terrible smell circulated around Westminster and many of the reporters and journalists who were on the ground reported feeling sick to the thick acrid smoke.

'Well, we now have to re-take each station' said Mike. Granville turned to the COBRA meeting committee and said 'we will do this in order, one at a time. We don't have enough men to properly secure each area.' So station by station they went to work, first surrounding and with the aide of overhead surveillance they were able to pinpoint exactly where the terrorists were. It would be another twenty four hours before the final station was clear. Again the devastation was immensely powerful to the naked eye. Helicopters were buzzing up and down the river Thames, Apache after Apache swirled overhead, hovering for long periods of time over the areas of attack. Chinooks landed on Parliament Square to unload personnel and also on Horse Guards Parade. Armoured vehicles were now outside every station, with hundreds of troops patrolling the area. London had become a war zone and in twenty four hours, a total disaster zone. For those who witnessed the Prime Minister's feeble reaction, their contempt for her grew by the second. An early day motion being proposed by the Conservative Party behind the scenes with the party's executive 1922 committee wanting to replace her with immediate effect. The motion would eventually be passed overwhelmingly and a new leader by the name of Harry Albrighton take over a week later. To think Mike would not sleep for 48 hours after the attacks, his adrenaline was running so high, he just could not lay still. Instead he found himself often walking around the attack sites at Westminster. Speaking to soldiers and civil servants. He just felt compelled to do something. He found an old sleeping bag and was regularly seen asleep on the floor of Downing St in the main Cabinet meeting room. General Granville, the Chief of Defence Staff (CDS), ordered food and water been made available to troops on the ground. Wellington barracks would be the main HQ for a temporary kitchen and mess tents.

With the phone lines down due to the terror attack, the public were indeed scared. It wasn't an everyday occurrence to witness live on TV, terrorists gunning down ordinary people. So the political war had just begun. Labour MPs were up in arms complaining about the heavy-handed nature of the Army response. The new Prime Minister knew Mike Scott was angry about the proposed defence cuts his predecessor had only floated a day or two before. So Albrighton asked Mike to do a round of interviews talking about the attacks. On TV show after TV show, Mike said the same thing, that we had indeed been lucky to have such good Army equipment and personnel to respond to the attacks. But time and again, Labour complained, totally ignorantly according to a whole range of polls and survey data. From DataPoll to TCM to ComGov, all pointed to the fact that an overwhelming eighty-five per cent of the public agreed with the government response and a further seventy-nine per cent gave their full support to the armed forces in general. This didn't come as easy reading for the weak PM, or that matter Chancellor. Who only forty-eight hours earlier had authorised cuts to the military that would see the Apache helicopter force cut by a third, with special forces units cut by a quarter and regular army numbers cut by an additional ten thousand personnel. The cuts were indeed postponed, in fact reversed. Defence spending actually went up in real terms for the first time in over two decades. To people like Mike who had seen first-hand the result of defence cuts, whilst in Bosnia when his vehicles broke down, didn't have enough spare parts or simply radios didn't work. Led to the phrase BOWMAN, which stood for 'Better Off With Map And Nokia', because the radio system was that unreliable. BOWMAN was actually the British Army radio communications system and it had a terrible reputation. Now being replaced by Project Morpheus, albeit slowly and without direction.

To Mike this timing was indeed brilliant, and his status was rising. The public liked his direct responses to the overzealous Labour calls for less force. Particularly when on one TV Interview he told the Labour MP to 'piss off'. Mike's popularity went up and up and up. With calls for him to be made the new Defence Secretary, a position he had long relished. And although he was coming up to retirement in a couple of years' time, he would eventually take up a seat in the House of Lords once it was rebuilt. But that is another story.

With Mike now at the helm of Defence spending and its newly appointed Defence Secretary, things were beginning to look up for a department that had for way too long been at the long end of a stick that kept getting longer. Defence was part and parcel of the UK fibre and backbone. For generations the British Army was described as the best in the world. That was no longer the case. It would take a full five years before the new spending kicked in and the benefits began to be felt, not just in terms of manpower, but in terms of new equipment, accommodation and pay.

Mike proposed that special forces soldiers be paid double, and their pensions doubled. The Chancellor nearly fell off his seat when Mike presented the proposals to him. Numerous arguments took place, but the new Prime Minister Albrighton wanted to send a clear signal to the world that the British were back and after such a devastating series of attacks, that there was a clear need to invest in the military for the long term. Tanks, yes, tanks that had been deemed 'unnecessary' were now back in fashion. Successive Prime Ministers had openly said that 'cyber' was the new way forward and that conventional warfare a thing of the past. This at the same time of huge numbers of Russian forces building up at the Ukraine border and then subsequently invading some years later in 2022. A few smart commentators and parliamentarians pointed out that quote 'a laptop cannot stop a tank' in evidence to the Defence Select Committee.

The political fallout from the terrorist attacks was immense. People were angry, the public were furious. Despite agreeing in large numbers that the government response was initially good, grieving families and there were literally thousands wanted blood. The terrorists were identified as being from Al-Saleem, an extremist terrorist group of Muslim origin founded by Osama Bin Ahmed. But these terrorists originated from Libya. The following days across Britain saw hundreds of mosques burned to the ground and hate crimes went through the roof. The police were reeling from their weak response to the attacks and the public were angry with them for not preventing this in the first place. Grieving family members were regularly interviewed on live TV, shouting for revenge and attacks against those responsible. It was a testy time for new Prime Minister Albrighton. He wanted to stamp his authority on the situation. He ordered the police to be highly visible around places of worship, but also around every mainland railway station the length and breadth of the land he ordered twenty-four hour armed police presence, he also ordered the Army to remain highly visible as they had now dug in and established regular patrols. He wanted to be seen as a strong leader and this enabled him to convey that image. It would take the police quite some time to make up the number of trained firearms units. So the Prime Minister ordered the Army remain on the streets at all main stations and around Parliament for the following months whilst things calmed down.

For Mike, what he wanted to do was understand how on earth these terrorists got into the country, and the weapons they had, how they managed to get hold of these? The Heads of MI6, MI5 and GCHQ were all summoned to the MoD on Whitehall for high level discussions and in a highly secure area. Roads were blocked off and there was a huge police presence to stop anyone from getting close to the meeting. Mike had been given the authority from PM Albrighton to conduct whatever was necessary to find out what had gone on. The PM also ordered an independent inquiry into the entire episode and asked a retired General to head up this investigation, with a remit to report back within a year. The report would be a damning affair for the government, in particular previous Prime Minister's were singled out for their lax immigration policies, poor funding of the armed forces and weak political will when it came to making Britain secure.

Mike sat in on various meetings with high ranking officials, all of whom were discussing what had happened. Talks went on for weeks. I mean the capital of London had been devastated and people wanted answers. In one such meeting, Mike said 'you mean to tell me, that these individuals, got in through the front door? They came in through Dover on the back of a lorry or on a dinghy, the kind we see on the news week in week out and then they were went about their plan to import weapons and personnel to conduct this operation?' 'Yes, that's correct' said the Intelligence Officer. 'Well, the first thing we are going to do is secure Dover Port. I want an Army presence there, I want twenty-four seven border staff presence to be increased tenfold, I want thermal imaging technology to scan every vehicle that enters the port. No one will get in to the UK via Dover without me knowing about it from this point on' said Mike. Mike couldn't believe it. How lax security was at Dover and along the South coast, but it wasn't just there, illegals were arriving via Ireland too on the West coast of England and Wales. 'I want to inspect what you are doing there tomorrow, have a helicopter pick me up from Whitehall and fly my down to Dover, we will spend the day there assessing what needs to be done. Have the Head of Border Force UK attend, along with the Police, and security services.' Said Mike. Mike was really stamping his authority on this mess; he wasn't going to have a free for all as had been the case for the previous couple of decades. And with Brexit imminent, this was perfect timing to reset national security. As for the National Security Advisor Max Trentworth, he was booted out of office. Mike had never taken to him. He was a yes man, and a bloody crap one at that. Mike couldn't stand yes men, he felt that they had 'no soul' as he would often exclaim.

Mike saw himself as a *Churchillian* type figure. Someone who was on a mission. And the mission was to save Britain from this kind of thing ever happening again. Prime Minister Albrighton was having different problems, from a faltering economy to rising costs of pensions. He was under pressure to curb spending and stimulate the economy. It would prove to be a controversial period in his Premiership as he drastically cut taxes on business, cut red tape and totally rolled out a brand-new tax system that revolutionised the way people pay tax. It was a godsend, within a couple of months, the economy began to pick up. Albrighton's popularity began to rise again. He was very well informed, and eloquent, he knew how to speak and when to speak. Unlike his predecessor who never had an opinion on anything, Albrighton was quite the contrary. He would rail against this or that, but the public seemed to like it. They liked the idea of a leader who was not afraid to say what he thought. That also appealed to Mike. On more than one occasion, Mike had to go to number ten *Downing Street* to explain what he was doing, and nine times out of ten, Albrighton agreed.

'Are we really sure this is the right thing to do Mike?' said Albrighton. 'Of course it is. We need to show the people and the world that UK PLC is not only open for business, but moreover, that we the government have complete control over who is coming and who is going.' Said Mike. Albrighton interrupted and said 'But wont this look a little heavy handed?' Mike shuffled his feet slightly, leant forward in his seat and pointed to the number of dead officially listed from the official report into the terror attack. 'We cannot afford to have this happen again. Business confidence was badly affected, a number of companies have put off investment plans until they can be certain that we are taking security seriously. I want us to show everyone, in particular those bastards who might be tempted to repeat this, that we will not allow it' said Mike. Albrighton sat back in his seat, 'right then, let's do it.' Albrighton picked up the phone to his new Chief of Staff and summoned him into the room. 'Cartwright' he said in a brisk tone, 'you do what Mike tells you to do and get this all through the civil service. I don't want any hold ups, excuses or delays. This project and any other like it must be pushed through at top speed.' 'I will mark it priority Sir.' Said Cartwright. 'Good' said Albrighton. Cartwright turned, picked up the file and left the PMs office promptly. Mike grinned and said. 'These measures are just what the port of Dover needs. It is an iconic location and one that says everything about who we are. Trust me.' Albrighton then thanked Mike for his time and asked him to provide regular status updates on a weekly basis so as to ensure everything was going to plan. Mike stood up and then walked out. Waiting for him in the lobby was his close protection officer. A former Army Captain who served with the Royal Fusiliers.

Meanwhile across town at the Institute of Directors, Secretary of State Esther McCarthy was giving a speech on workforce engagement of all things, when she was rudely interrupted by hecklers from the back of the room. 'We won't allow Tory scum to stop people entering Britain. It's a free country!' they shouted. Security promptly ushered the two out of the conference hall. McCarthy didn't know what to say. She hadn't a clue what they were on about and just shrugged her shoulders. Once her presentation was over, she took questions from the assembled press corp. First one from *The Mercury* flew in, 'so Madam Secretary, do you really think make Britain a fortress is going to stop another terror attack?' Esther looked puzzled. She replied with some gusto, but caution saying 'we take Britain's safety and security very seriously and no options are off the table when it comes to protecting the public.' The *DBC news* reporter chipped in, 'will the Secretary of State confirm that it is now government policy to screen every individual entering the UK?' Esther again looking somewhat puzzled replied, 'I thought we were supposed to be talking about employee engagement today, not national security. If you want to talk security I suggest you speak to the Home or Defence Secretary.' The audience rumbled. Clearly amused by her quick response. Esther left the stage, walking out through the back and waiting for her security escort, off to her car. Once inside she said to her advisor 'what was that all about?' her advisor replied 'just in, looks like the PM has approved Mike Scott's security measures, which includes using the Army to totally search everything that comes in via Dover port.' 'The press will have a field day over that, take me to No.10 – I want to hear this from the PM myself.' Esther was a bit angry that she hadn't been told about this impending policy. She wasn't the only one, the PM himself was angry. In his office he was shouting down the phone to his Chief of Staff, 'what the bloody hell do you mean, you don't know? What do I pay you for? Well bloody sort it out.' It was becoming clear to Albrighton that there was a leak in his government, either civil servant, most likely or disgruntled political staff. To Harry Albrighton, this was nothing new, all throughout his political career he had faced numerous events like this. But this was different, the speed of the leak, was what concerned him. And more importantly it undermined the cohesion, let alone state security, if such private information is released without approval.

Mike on the other hand had no problems with his new command. Having been a senior commanding officer of a prestigious regiment, he knew the importance of leadership. Moreover, being seen to be doing rather than faffing about. His aims were clear as Defence Secretary: secure Britain and prepare for War. Of course he had no intention of going to war, rather the contrary. He wanted peace. All his military career he had been employed by various governments of all political colours to sue for peace. Invariably, it took acts of war to secure peace, but to Mike he knew that the country must feel safe. So he got to work by establishing a new Defence Advisory Board. Comprising of existing members of the military and a number of retired officers, intelligence and otherwise. Friends of Mike whom he could trust. Trust was vital in matters of national security. For Mike his closest friends like Ted Maguire, who was now in his early seventies, still had a spring in his step. Mike employed him as a special advisor. Years of work in both the Royal Marines and MI6, let alone working with Mike in Bosnia on security matters. Mike knew he could trust him implicitly. The new Defence board met once per week in Whitehall, in the newly refurbished MoD building. Mike quickly forgot about Cakebread, although on more than one occasion actually considered hiring him as his Chief of Staff after he found out how badly he had been treated. But we will return to that later. Meanwhile and somewhat Ironically, Mike had been against such a costly refurb of the MoD, preferring rather that the funds be spent on procuring a fleet of brand-new main battle tanks. But that decision was before his time. Mike was lucky however, he had a new pot of money available for him to spend. And spend he did. Wisely. He knew that the previous National Security Advisor was forever banging on about cyber warfare. But the reality as Mike knew, was that boots on the ground always saved the day. So the first thing Mike did was to instruct the Army to increase its regular strength to one hundred and ten thousand troops, with an additional one hundred thousand in reserve. To Mike, strength in numbers was vital. Mike loved military parades; each week he made an effort to get about the country visiting each and every barracks to watch the troops on parade. He wanted an elite fighting force, made up of professionals. He also made sure that they were well paid, fed and resourced. Mike had Boeing and Lockheed Martin fly in at short notice. Mike told them quite clearly that the British Armed Forces now had a requirement for one hundred brand new Chinook heavy lift helicopters, two hundred brand new Apache Gunships, and ten additional Wedgetail Early Warning Aircraft. But unlike previous orders, he wanted this equipment delivered within a year. Mike got on the phone to his counterpart in the United States and surprisingly had the backing of the Americans. They were well aware of the size of the order Mike had just placed, but more importantly wanted to get Britain's military up to strength as fast as possible. Mike had jumped out of countless troop transport aircraft being a Para. He had also personally used the Warrior Infantry Fighting Vehicle. Which was ancient and needed massive upgrades. So, Mike spoke with BAE Systems and placed an order for seven thousand Bradley Armoured Fighting Vehicles. The kind the US Army used on all its most recent operations. Mike wanted parity. He knew that the British military had often been described as 'the borrowers' by the Americans, forever asking to borrow equipment. Mike wanted to put an end to that and ensure that the British military would be able to stand on its own two feet for the long term. All this spending was raising political eyebrows, with opposition MPs criticising defence spending, claiming more should be spent on welfare. Mike fundamentally disagreed on countless TV interviews, saying, he had helped more working-class people into employment throughout his military career than any policy wonk from the DWP. His comments went down well with the military and veterans alike. Survey data appeared to suggest that a majority of the public agreed with the new spending spree, some sixty-three per cent of people agreeing that 'defence was now a priority.' But to Mike, he was a fair man. He didn't want to forget the Royal Navy, who had borne the brunt of cuts in the previous defence review. So, Mike went about a lightning visit to Portsmouth and Plymouth naval bases respectively. Inspecting the newly refitted Type 45 Destroyers, who had just had their TacTom Harpoon launchers re-installed, along with brand new turbines. Mike wanted to avoid repeating the same mistakes of previous procurement debacles. 'So', he said to BAE Systems who were to build the new Type 26 Frigates that they had to have the very best turbines, and weapons systems out there. Mike ordered the Treasury to find the funds for thirty Type 26 Frigates. A huge order to industry insiders. It caused a stir; this was a massive contract for the ship building industry. Mike wanted the first three ships available within a year. Despite protests from contractors, the first new ship was launched a year later. It was possible to do more and Mike kept pushing the timetable forward for ship deliveries. He wanted five ships per year to roll off the slip way. The Royal Navy absolutely loved Mike for what he had done. Single handed reversing years of cuts to the fleet. In fact, both the RAF and the Army were equally delighted. There was a buzz around most military bases, finally the military was being invested in. And taken far more seriously than by the four previous administrations put together and Mike made sure people knew that. On one TV show saying quite simply that 'Britain could now be proud of its military for the first time in two decades.'

Mike found himself reading books on *Churchill, Eisenhower* and various other world leaders. One thing rung true and reverberated throughout Mike's inner self. The need to deliver for the people. He knew he was Defence secretary and not Prime Minister. But he wanted to make sure people remembered his legacy and would say, 'that was due to Colonel Scott'. Mike's wife launched countless ships for the Navy, along with a host of other dignitaries. On counter terror raids Mike had oversight. The Special Forces were employed every time there was an arrest. Wearing police uniforms and balaclavas, repeated TV news shows showed burly men, bundling suspects into the back of police vans. Legally mind you. But with a bit of brute force and ignorance. There was now a change of attitude, not just from the government, but rather the public mood had changed. People wanted an end to terror. The problem was, this could never be achieved and Mike knew that. He knew all his efforts would do is change perception in the media, which was powerful. Mike knew being a politician that the power of the media as a weapon was infinite. Mike launched countless advertising campaigns on the TV and press to advertise the military recruitment and ultimately buy favour with the media. His plan worked. The PR department at the MoD had been monitoring year on year an increase in positive news stories amongst key media partners. Mike quipped to the Prime Minister 'who said advertising doesn't work?' It was an incredibly busy time in his life and family was important to him. His family didn't see much of him as he was often away. His second wife and their four children were used to that. His children from his first marriage now had children of their own and he had become a proud grandad.

Ted Maguire said to Mike 'you really need more intelligence on the situation. You could do with knowing a lot more about what our enemies are up to.' 'And how do you propose we do that?' said Mike, 'Well' said Ted. 'You need to infiltrate and capture a number of suspects abroad. We need to know what they are planning.' Mike replied curtly, 'and the Americans? What will they say? They have been doing just that since 9/11 and kept everyone out of it.' He went on, 'the minute our teams capture someone in the field, they are ordered to hand them over for interrogation. Either shipped out to Guantanamo or Bangkok. Either way, we don't get a look in'. 'Well' said Ted, 'perhaps it is time we said nothing.' But Mike looked up from his desk, 'they will find out, look at the leaks here in this government, we can't keep anything secret.' Ted stood up out of his seat, 'whilst I was in Hong Kong in the 1980s, stationed there, we captured and interrogated a number of Vietnamese boat people smugglers. Totally illegal, no one knew about it, but what this gave us was invaluable Intel on the movements of traffickers, shipments and middle men. We intercepted countless ships before they even entered territorial waters and sent them packing. If we can do that and get away with it, then we can do the same in Syria, Iraq, Lebanon, Libya, you name it.' Mike wasn't happy, he knew this was like opening a can of worms, moreover, he would need people he could implicitly trust. For that he agreed with Ted that a small team of nine men and one woman would be selected. Five from Mike, five from Ted. Ultimately with the aim of launching a rendition programme out of the aforementioned countries. Flying suspects to the Kalahari Desert in Botswana. Botswana had been an ally and regular military partner of the British Army. Mike knew that they needed somewhere off the map, the desert was a perfect place, no risk of satellite coverage, limited population centre. They hatched a plan to begin syphoning funds off to black ops anti-terror teams managed by MI6. With the funds, small aircraft, helicopters, jeeps, trucks, tents and local personnel were employed. The Kalahari bushmen were renowned for their survival skills, and the Botswana Defence Force, were surprisingly effective when it came to interrogation techniques. But Mike wanted to keep this operation in house, he didn't want the locals involved, in case word got out about what they were doing. Ted and Mike both had friends in the Jordanian Intelligence Service the GID. These guys were expert at getting a confession. They didn't ever torture suspects, rather, use them, a little like the mafia did with its informers. Mike and Ted knew they needed Arab speakers, so the Jordanian Intelligence contact Ted had from the past was contacted. A small team out of Amman was recruited to help out with this black ops mission. Posing as tourists in Botswana, they like their British counterparts flew in and out of the country on a regular basis, taking domestic flights up to Maun where they were transferred by jeep into the desert. Ted had agreed a slush fund with Mike designed to pay off local officials, in particular, Botswana military to ensure that they wouldn't 'disturb' the operation whilst in progress. It worked perfectly well. The size of the camp grew by the week. Eventually almost transforming into a tumbleweed type village, with solar power, running water, you name it. The only time Kalahari bushmen were employed, was to watch over the camp when it was empty. Ensuring the wildlife and would be looters kept well out.

Mike told Ted that he would have to keep at arm's length from this operation, but he would mark the dossier as beyond top secret for the PMs eyes only. 'You did what?!' said Albrighton. 'Let me get this straight, just so I am clear. You opened up our own Guantanamo style camp in the middle of the Kalahari Desert. Which is where by the way?' said Albrighton. 'Yep' said Mike. 'We aren't torturing suspects, rather converting them for information. The reality is, without UpToDate intelligence, we will never win the war on terror. Only you and I have access to this information' said Mike. 'Well, let's keep this quiet, I don't want it mentioned again, if anything happens or the press find out, I don't know anything about it.' Said Albrighton. 'Fine' said Mike, 'we will crack on.' As Mike stood to leave the PMs Office, the PM said one final time 'you are sure about this aren't you?', 'never more certain' said Mike. Mike left the office walking back across Whitehall to the MoD building, as he did, protestors were outside Downing Street, protesting the military, complaining to the media that the British military was turning the UK into a police state. When Mike was stopped by a *UK News* reporter, he said quite simply in reply to a question 'utter tosh' and walked on. To the amusement of the assembled media, who had become familiar with Mike's quotes and speeches. It strangely took the sting out of the protestors, with reporters now playing down the mob outside No.10 as a 'gaggle of complainers, with not a good word for the British military.' Prime Minister Albrighton, laughed, when he heard what Mike had said. He always managed to get himself out of a jam.

Some years went past and having retired as an MP and now being a new member of the House of Lords, Lord Scott of Kingston upon Thames, rarely made an appearance in the chamber. Only on important government matters did he dare to venture into the temporary Parliament which was in the QE Centre. Often, before doing so, he would reminisce on the massive painting of the battle of Trafalgar just outside the old chamber and take in the sheer magnificence of the painting. The attention to detail, the wrecks, the men, the smoke. To Mike, this reminded him of a time when Britain was great, when Britain won. Moreover, it made him feel nostalgic to reflect upon conflicts past. Modern Britain had changed so much that there were times when he didn't recognise what was going on. From the ever-increasing Somali communities in London, to the Pakistani towns up north. Mike often asked himself what the strategic value of having as he put it 'large numbers of Islamic soldiers potentially, allowed into the UK, only to turn on us at the very first opportunity.' Mike was privy to the latest intel, he had read the reports about the child abuse scandals throughout the country by Pakistani men. He had read about the Somali gangs pushing drugs and their proceeds going to fund Al Saleem. He had read about the abuse of power in Mosques by Imams who called for Jihad. To Mike, all of this was dangerous and represented a clear and present danger to the UK. Mike was relentless in his pursuit of these individuals. The terror attacks on London had given him not only a licence to operate, but the public support and more importantly funding to do what he wanted. Mike stood up during one debate in the House of Lords and openly said 'we must seek to reduce our reliance on migrants coming to the UK who potentially pose a grave threat to our way of life. Consideration should be given to a blanket ban on such nations until such time as the situation is more clear.' To howls of 'racist' and 'fascist' even at Mike's age, despite his fantastic reputation, there were left wing extremists even in the House of Lords, who launched repeated tirades against Mike. Communists they claimed to be in private, Mike's detractors regularly stirred trouble, politically speaking in the temporary House of Lords. To which Mike brushed aside accusations as 'froth'. Much to the amusement of a former Admiral, now Lord Irving of Spithead. Lord Irving was a 'simple sailor' as he put it himself. And although a member of the Labour party, he was defiantly patriotic. He had voted for Brexit and always stood up for the military in the Lords and often in the press, despite now being in his early seventies. He found the need to speak out 'his duty' as he put it. Openly he had praised Colonel Scott for his renewal of the Royal Navy and military as a whole. Recognising the strategically important procurement Mike had overseen. Mike was that impressed by the record of Lord Irving, that he asked the Prime Minister to let Irving join Mike's defence board committee. To which PM Albrighton agreed. Lord Irving knew his stuff and during the Libya conflict had been a fierce critic of the then Prime Minister David Norris, not because of the military involvement, rather the fact that 'Dave' was looking to cut the military at the same time as embarking on a military operation. On more than one occasion Irving went public, angrily denouncing the stupidity of PM Norris. Mike had agreed in private at the time. It was uncanny really. Here you now had three Lords, from three different political parties, all members of the same committee on Defence. Lord Maguire a Liberal Democrat, Lord Irving a Labour member and Lord Scott from the Conservatives. Who would have thought it even remotely possible only a decade earlier? As mentioned, it was later discovered that the terrorists who attacked London were all Libyan. Something coincidental or just a random fact? The Libyans were out to get anyone responsible for the overthrow of their leader little did Jack know.

Mike's agenda was gaining momentum around Westminster on the otherhand, not only with hard liners, but moderates too were beginning to like the direction in which the Conservative government was travelling. Headlines in newspapers rang out endorsements of Mike's initiatives like 'Secretary of State gets support for blanket ban,' 'migrant numbers to be slashed', 'Minister says no more'. Mike's remit had grown, it felt like anything to do with

Defence and Security was now his. Much to the annoyance of the Home Secretary, a relative newcomer, but someone with ambition, who fancied himself as PM. Home Secretary Bashir was a relative rising star in the party, but Mike felt he didn't have the strength or for that matter backbone required to enforce order on the chaos that had ensued out of the terror attacks. When the terror attacks had taken place at the time Bashir was pretty useless, a little like the PM Rebecca Matthews at the time. The only difference was the Tory party had recognised the need to increase its presence with ethnic minorities and it was felt that Bashir was the 'best option' for the time being. It was clear who was calling the shots though. Mike Scott. Not only did he have the ear of Harry Albrighton, he regularly met with Prince Richard. Richard being a former Army officer himself took a great interest in the goings on at the MoD in the aftermath of Westminster. He wanted to ensure that he would provide whatever assistance he could to make a difference 'moving forward'. 'God the PC Brigade bullshit we have to put up with is beyond the joke' said Mike, sipping at his pint of London Pride. 'Well, you think that's bad, last week I had to open a fucking community centre' said Richard. 'If it wasn't for all the reliance on Saudi oil and investment, we wouldn't have a thing to do with the Arab world. We could shut up shop and tell them to fuck off.' Mike nodded. 'Yep, but they are our allies and we need to work together, so let's try to look at the positives.' Mike said. 'God even you are sounding like one of them now' said Richard. 'Ha! Piss off!' said Mike. Richard laughed out loud. 'Let's take a ride' said Richard, 'I want to see the latest Apache helicopter'. 'Hang on a minute, I haven't finished my drink' said Mike. 'I will get one to fly over now and land at Wellington Barracks.' 'Ok sure, get them here quick.' Mike looked a little out of sorts, although, calm and casual as usual he said 'I take it you have a reason to look at the helo?' said Mike. 'Why yes, when I was in the Army, we had the Apache, but that was the old version, I want to see the latest variant' said Richard. 'If you insist, your highness.' Said Mike. To the British people, the Royal family was still a very popular institution. Although, slightly more glamorised and politically correct, it had managed to keep up with the times albeit with a few scandals on the way. It has to be said that Richard's marriage to an American movie star made him the toast of the town. He was already immensely popular, but she made them, A-listers. Mike knew the amount of terror threats the country faced, and Prince Richard was the number one target, having served in Iraq and Libya. Mike had allocated two special forces soldiers to Richard's personal protection squad. In total Richard had some twenty men and women at his side whenever he stepped out. The difference was this was rarely seen. The British government opting for a softly, softly does it approach to Royal security. They were a brand after all, and a brand that represented Britain. Mike wanted to make Richard a poster boy for the military and managed to sign up Prince Richard for the latest round of advertising campaigns, designed to increase recruitment manning levels.

The Apache buzzed overhead, with the noise of its Rolls Royce engines purring, the helicopter swirled in the air, low, and calm over Westminster. This had become a regular sight and landing at Wellington Barracks with its newly painted landing pad was nothing out of the ordinary. Mike and Richard jumped into the blacked-out Range Rover waiting for them. Armour plated, bullet and gas proof. This vehicle was a beast. They drove out of Westminster round the corner to Bird Cage Walk and then left in the Barracks main gate. The helicopter crew were standing outside of their helicopter inspecting the aircraft. A ground crew had also met them and was beginning to refuel the bird. Armed sentries stood at the main gate that Mike and Richard just passed through. Saluting once they knew who was inside. Out stepped Richard first, then Mike followed the other side. Their close protection officers fanning out around them at a relative safe distance. The Commanding officer of Wellington Barracks appeared, 'hello Sir, pleasure to see you again' he said. 'Very good Major, carry on' said Mike. 'Let's have a look inside' said Richard. They walked up to the open canopy and the pilot, a young Lieutenant smiled. 'Good evening Sir' he said. 'I hear you are here to take a look at the Apache?' 'That's right' said Richard. 'Ok well hop in'. Richard proceeded to clamber aboard, carefully managing to avoid the main panel which said do not touch written all over it. 'Looks impressive. Compared to the variant I used, this is far better.' Richard uttered. Mike turned to him and said 'we have spent a small fortune on getting hold of the very best available in the market.' Richard proceeded to get out of the helicopter; he stood around talking to the pilots and crew. Mike too wanted to hear about the performance of the aircraft and this gave him ample first-hand insight into that. The helipad was pretty busy, with the royal party, Mike and various security staff. There was a small tow truck, designed to tow the helicopters around the landing site. On it there was a sign '*Where Arrows Meet*' for the towing point. On this occasion there was no need to manoeuvre the helicopter, but it was often the case that the landing pad was used as a practice parade ground, so the bird had to be moved from time to time when on the ground to make space for the assembled squaddies on parade practice.

Richard got back into his Range Rover, and the convoy sped off into the distance. Richard was heading to his residence at High Street Kensington, Kensington Palace. Mike got into a staff car and was driven home to his flat just next to the Mall. As Mike sat in his chair sipping some French cognac, he reflected on what had been a very busy day. But immensely enjoyable. He felt that he wasn't just doing a job, but that it was vital that he continued to serve the country in whatever way he could.

The vibration of the mobile phone rang out, Mike turned in his bed to the phone to switch off the alarm. It had woken him, feeling a little groggy from the night before. He got up and went over to the bathroom to take a shower. As the water ran over him, he felt alive like never before. Once dry, he got dressed and his phone rang out loud. It was the PM. Wanting an update on operations. Mike said he would be in the office in half an hour and would then meet him at No.10 with his latest reports. 'Before you do, I need you to do an interview with the *DBC news*. They are doing a piece on torture for Panorama and I want you to head up our response' said Albrighton. Mike sighed, 'are you sure?'. '100 per cent. And make sure you don't mention anything about the Kalahari.' Said Albrighton.

The *DBC news* studio on Milbank was modern, it had an air of IKEA about it, new décor, furniture and what have you. The receptionist who greeted Mike as he entered was a young woman, about twenty-five. 'Tea or coffee for you?' she said. 'No thanks'. Mike replied. As he sat in the reception, he watched the *DBC news* live on the screen with subtitles. He was reading about the economy; the latest figures showed the economy had grown by 0.9 per cent in the last quarter. A coup for Prime Minister Albrighton who had advocated tax cuts. 'Proof our policies are working for ordinary people' said the Prime Minister on the television. Mike laughed and as he did another young woman walked into the reception and said 'Lord Scott? This way please.' She escorted him into the interviewing room, cameras and lighting were all setup, it was kind of a weird setting, but Mike didn't think too much of it. The interviewer was a well-known ball breaker from Panorama. Never satisfied with the status quo, always after an angle, always wanting to 'get' ministers. 'So, I bet you're happy' she said in a sly tone. 'What?' said Mike. 'You know, the economy, I bet you and your Tory chums are all jumping up and down with glee?' 'Not quite. Erm, is this interview going to be conducted in the same manner?

If so I can tell you right away, I won't stand for it. If you want to ask me questions, then ask away, but please, keep the bitchy comments to yourself.' Talk about put someone in their place. Mike was expert at that, and hence why PM Albrighton loved him. He was to the point, cutting and yet still strangely affable. 'Your funding is up for review isn't it?' said Mike. 'Pardon?' she replied. 'Yes, I remember now, my colleague was telling me how the funding review for the *DBC* was going.' And that was all Mike said on the matter. 'Ok right let's get started. So, Secretary of State for Defence, Lord Scott, please can you give us an outline of how the war on terror is going?' Mike began to reel off-key milestones, achievements, from military numbers, new equipment, patrols, presence at borders, arrests. Overall, Mike painted a sound picture of government policy. He came across really well, like someone you wanted to hear more from. He was great at conveying a message, he commanded authority and it just flowed from him when he spoke. 'And what do you know about torture?' the interviewer said abruptly. 'Quite a lot' said Mike. She looked shocked. 'What do you mean?' she said. 'Well, you see, I was kind of a torturer in Bosnia.' Said Mike. 'How do you mean?' she replied. 'Well, when I was there, I had to protect the local Muslim, civilian population from massacre. The only way I could do that was, when we captured enemy soldiers, in particular their intelligence officers, we would often give them a truth serum to help them loosen up and speak' said Mike. 'Oh my word, isn't this against international conventions?!' said the interviewer. 'Possibly, but then again so is genocide.' Said Mike. Mike said with a straight look on his face. The reporter knew, she wouldn't get anywhere with this line of attack. If anything, it made her look stupid to even question what he had done. 'Things aren't always black and white you see. Sometimes, when the shells are falling, bombs are going off, people are dying, left right and centre. Action has to be taken. We never tortured anyone physically, i.e. no violence. We just used truth serums.' And they worked. On more than one occasion, we prevented an atrocity from taking place at a local food station. Until you have been in that position yourself, you can never know how you will react.' 'Have you ever killed someone?' She probed. 'Yes, on more than one occasion'. Said Mike. 'How do you live with yourself' she exclaimed. 'Rather well actually.' Mike was unmoved, he answered the questions openly and to a degree honestly. He knew that the government line was being tested here. Countless suspects had been shipped off to Guantanamo, the reporter wanted to press Mike and see what she could get out of him. But he gave away nothing. If anything, the interview, made him look like a true leader. Being in his mid sixties didn't matter, people wanted age and experience over youth and drama. The public had been surveyed after the interview and a majority of fifty-eight per cent agreed with the statement 'the British government is looking after the country well'. The remains and wreckage that was Westminster, Houses of Parliament was still being removed. Construction workers had been drafted in and the massive project to rebuild was slowly underway. Unlike the previous renovation of Big Ben which was a farce and far too slow. This rebuilding project had been fully funded to the tune of ten billion pounds. Large sums coming from the private sector, with numerous companies offering skills, expertise and labour for free. The designs of the new Parliament were impressive. It was to be very similar in terms of look and feel to the previous, but with the difference that office space and meeting rooms were incorporated. The whole structure would be ten feet higher to incorporate additional floors. Moreover, the security and design of the place would have to change. Ministers wanted to make the entrances bomb proof. Which would be difficult. But extra layers of security were added and Parliament Square was able to keep traffic flowing freely. Mike regularly went down to the site, with his hard hat on, he surveyed the plans and watched as the foundations were installed. Rebuilding such a grand

and ornate building went to the leading architects at the time *Foster & Partners*. Lord Foster was an incredible architect. With his new designs, he incorporated the very best in air conditioning, which, to anyone who has visited Parliament in summer knows all too well, is unbearable at times. The same was true of the front, main entrance to Portcullis House. Construction crews had managed to remove the mangled mess, of steel and concrete that lay charred over the stairways. They had decided that the best option was to completely knock down the building and heavy diggers were brought in to start the process of breaking down piece by piece, the dark structure. The plans estimated at the time that the rebuild would take at least four years. Mike wanted it done quicker. So, he invited the architects of the Freedom Tower in New York to visit and give their opinions. Granted this wasn't a military matter, Mike had to tread carefully. But he did have the blessing of the Prime Minister so he pressed ahead nevertheless. The same was true of the main line railway stations which were now massive construction sites also. They still had massive military presences, which made the site look like a war zone. But these arteries into London were vital to keep the city moving. So, whilst the reconstruction was agreed and well underway. The Prime Minister wanted to ensure London was at the centre of the world, and ordered Crossrail three, four and five to take place. Huge infrastructure projects, designed to give London a brand-new railway system that would be unrivalled the world over. The costs were enormous, but to Prime Minister Albrighton, they were absolutely vital to the success and prosperity of the nation. A giant search light was placed next to the sight of Parliament and lit up every night into the sky. There were also images of the Houses of Parliament lit up and projected on to the Shell building. Mike was sure of one thing, that the media would be essential in the war on terror, but also on the renewal of the brand image that was UK PLC.

When it came to the strategic threat assessment, it was concluded with the confirmation that the terrorists had originated from Libya. Moreover, that their funding, training and resources also came from that area. Mike wanted this changing, so did the PM and cabinet. So, Mike came out with some radical thinking. Not only was domestic security important, he wanted to reduce the UKs reliance on oil from the Middle East. So overnight LNG deals with the likes of Qatar were not renewed, with the UK instead opting to import vast quantities of Shale Gas from the United States. When it came to petrol, the government wanted to wean off the Arab oil so began a range of initiatives with big public subsidies and funding, such as electric vehicle production, charging points. Hydrogen powered vehicles and refuelling stations. The scale of the project was vast. It had been prior to the terror attacks quite miniscule with for example only a handful of petrol stations in the capital offering hydrogen refuelling. Now the government would pay for one hundred per cent coverage. To small hydrogen powered firms this was a god send, but to the automotive industry too, the government offered very generous tax-free subsidies and offers to manufacturers and consumers alike. With a massive advertising campaign across the internet, press and TV promoting hydrogen power. Critics initially wrote off the ideas, but this was really going places. Immediately, the automotive industry reported a substantial amount of interest. Not only were hydrogen powered cars cheaper, they were cheaper to run and you paid no tax on them. After a year pretty much every manufacturer began to offer a range of hydrogen powered vehicles for sale. Mike got the credit for the initiative. It was his idea after all. PM Albrighton got the credit from the green lobby who called his moves 'truly incredible'. Market share of hydrogen cars was up to fifty-two per cent after the first year. New car registrations were rising year on year, and for the first-time air pollution recorded a minor fall in levels of nitrogen dioxide. Solar panel initiatives were also launched, with all of

Whitehall covered in solar panels, and the new Parliament buildings totally energy self-sufficient. Additional nuclear power plants were ordered by the Prime Minister, he wanted to the UK to be one hundred per cent energy independent. It was an incredible sight in the temporary Parliament that was the Queen Elizabeth conference centre in Westminster, there was agreement across all sides of the house. Politicians of all colours were in agreement. The US Shale Gas imports were a temporary solution to provide for Gas needs, whilst the nuclear plants were built. North Sea Gas supplies had been in decline for the past decade, so the US was the only option left. The time line for building nuclear was long, slow and often tedious. Mike again wasn't happy and wanted things done far quicker. After meeting with the PM, they agreed that twenty brand new nuclear power plants were required and would be fully funded. Construction contracts were handed to British firms, given the political controversy of handing previous contracts to Chinese and French organisations. This would mark a huge shift in policy. Something that really would put a lot of pressure on Arab states to clamp down on extremist activities. They had watched and seen first-hand the British response to the terror attacks and they were embarrassed about what had happened. They offered to stump up funds for the construction of power plants, but the PM refused. He said 'we have to build these ourselves. We have to make a statement to the world on the future of Britain.' It went down well. Most Brits who were surveyed during the first year of construction agreed seventy-two per cent that 'energy independence was essential for the UK'. Mike took a helicopter ride down to Dungeness to see first-hand the construction taking place. The site was enormous, as the helicopter circled overhead, the sheer scale of the project was impressive. The old site had been taken down and a new build reactor was being put in place. The Merlin helicopter landed on the site, with the site manager racing up to the helicopter. 'Hello Minister, thank you for coming' he said. 'Not a problem, we're here to inspect progress.' Said Mike. As they walked about the site, Mike realised that he knew nothing about construction or for that matter nuclear material. What he knew was timetables, routine and practicalities. After a fifteen-minute update from the site manager, Mike and his team climbed back aboard the helicopter for a short flight back to London. En route, the pilot reported engine problems and had to land in a field in Kent. Mike was not amused. The Merlin helicopter had old engines, despite being from Rolls Royce, it was clear that they needed replacing. Mike got onto his satellite phone to MoD procurement and said, 'make sure you order new, more powerful engines to replace the existing ones on the Merlin fleet. And not just like for like, I want fifty per cent extra spare engines.' Once another support helicopter arrived, Mike climbed aboard and took off for Whitehall. The Merlin and her maintenance crew now working on the fix. Eventually after an hour, the Merlin took off again and limped back to base for deep maintenance.

One thing that also changed after the terror attacks was the number of times senior ministers had to check in. Typically, three times throughout the day, they had to now, send a message to a security operative who logged their location and what they were doing. At the height of the terror attacks, when certain ministers were sought after, they were nowhere to be found. For such critical people to be AWOL represented a huge security dilemma for the British government. So, this rig moral of now checking in was becoming a bit of a faff for many of the ministers, particularly those who were not from a traditional military background. Quite the contrary, they found the process, boring and didn't really appreciate the gravity of the situation. So, the Prime Minister decided that in the event that a full COBRA committee could not be assembled and a vote or decisions not taken by senior ministers, indeed authority would fall to civil servants to make decisions, just as General Granville had done. Life at number ten Downing Street was always a buzz with people coming and going, since the attacks the barricades had gone up. Sand bags lined the street and it did very much look like a scene from World War Two. PM Albrighton was acutely aware of how this looked to the assembled media. Regularly congregating to the side of the main entrance, bickering and now openly criticising the height of the barricades because often their view of the main door at number ten was now blocked. PM Albrighton ordered the sandbags to be taken down immediately outside the front door. Saying that it was 'unsightly'. When Mike heard about this decision, he laughed out loud. He knew politics well, he knew the power of the media and he also knew that this state of war could not last forever. All but essential barricade/ sand bag cover would be removed. Even the Panther armoured liaison vehicle parked at the front and rear of Downing Street was removed to the adjacent side streets. The PM wanted to the visible eye at least be seen to be scaling back military presence at number ten. The media bought it. Which was exactly what the PM wanted. A *DBC news* journalist was overheard saying live on lunchtime news 'Reporting live here at ten Downing Street, we have just witnessed the Army removing large barricades and sandbags from the area. With military vehicles being removed.' Albrighton wanted to promote the UK like never before, he knew that the tourism sector had taken a massive blow after the attacks. So, he launched a brand-new advertising campaign designed to promote the very best of London. 'Try to imagine the opening scene in the movie *Goldfinger*' he said, 'you know, when the plane is flying along Miami beach with a sign in tow, 'welcome to Miami'. We want the glitz and glamour of London to shine through and we are employing the top creative and media agencies out there to put this together for us. Not just a one off, I want a series of ads. I want London's skyline to be the focal point' said Albrighton. With that, the PM was routinely in countless meeting with ad men in an effort to put together the very best in class of advert for the capital city. Mike on the other hand was preoccupied with GCHQ. He had been on a mission to totally shake it up in light of the attacks. One of the problems he had was that previous governments had gone out of their way to politicise the security services. Mike wanted an end to that. With no more calls for diversity or other politically correct language. Mike wanted the best and he had none of it when it came to the looney left lobby groups. Upon a trip to Gloucester to visit the newly refurbed GCHQ he sat down and spoke to the Director in charge of the entire facility. 'So, tell me' he said. 'What are you lot doing here? Playing computer games? Or actually intercepting terrorist transmissions?' You see, Mike wasn't too happy with GCHQ, because in the run up to the attacks it appears that they actually had raw data that pointed to at least seven of the attackers. But this wasn't followed up on and actually in one case the red warning lights should have been flashing but no one actioned anything. 'I want to see wholesale change here' said Mike. 'This simply isn't good enough. We cannot have a situation whereby you are getting all this funding, have all these staff and are completely unable to even pick up the basics. We tested you last week with a number of dummy transcripts and intercepts and your teams didn't have a clue?' he went on 'what on earth is going on here? This really isn't good enough.' 'Lord Scott, I can assure you my staff.' Before he could finish Mike jumped in 'spare me the pleasantries. I want you to provide me with a plan by this time next week of what you propose you are going to do to change all of this. I mean practical steps that your department can and will take, that can be implemented rapidly.' The Director looked down to the ground, gulped and sat back in his chair. 'I am not sure you fully appreciate what we do here' he said. 'No, perhaps not. But that is irrelevant. What you are doing isn't working. Make it work, or you are out. And don't think you are getting any golden goodbyes or payoffs. The new government directive is failure is not to be rewarded.' With that Mike stood up, walked to the door where his security team was waiting outside. Then he quickly moved to the exit, a walk across the carpark to the helicopter. Mike had ordered the pilot to land in the GCHQ carpark. Since his last break down in a Merlin and with the engine upgrades still taking place. Mike commandeered a brand-new Little Bird helicopter. It was small enough to fit into tight spaces, ideal for Mike; he liked the idea of choppering in and out. He used to do that all the time in the Paras. Nothing had changed in some respects; the only difference was he now wore a suit. Which reminded him; he had an appointment on *Savile Row* for a new dinner jacket and needed to move quick sharp back to Whitehall. Once the Little Bird touched down on Horse Guards Parade. Mike's other security team was waiting for him. Their blacked-out Land Rovers engines were running. He walked briskly to the car, got in and said 'Savile Row please.' And the tailors Henderson and sons, he opted for a single-breasted dinner jacket and funnily enough, whilst he sipped on some fine Scottish whisky, he was persuaded to get measured up for a new three-piece suit. Double-breasted of course. Mike was old school in that regard. As he leant back in the chair, a young man looked in through the window. It was Jack Cakebread, Mike knew him from his days at the Defence think tank, *UKDO*. Jack was a civilian, not an ounce of military experience, yet, incredibly well read on military matters, equipment in particular and tactics. Jack was more of a political strategist; he had worked in advertising and had a number of smaller roles in politics but nothing substantial. He waved through the window. Mike signalled back for him to come in. The main door was locked. Henderson and sons always locked up when private clients, extremely rich and famous were on site. Mike just happened to be very important. So that was good enough. The door opened, a tall, broad set security officer waved in Jack and asked who he was and if it was ok to pat him down. Immediately Mike sparked up 'no need for that Steve. Let him in' Jack walked straight up to Mike and hand extended shook hands. 'Good to see you Mike, it's been a long time. The last time I saw you was on the Eurostar in Paris, when you were with you son for a trip to the museums, remember? Oh, that was a good two years ago.' 'Ah yes, good memory' said Mike. For Jack, he was disappointed. Because whilst at the *UKDO*, Mike had promised him he would 'take him with him' once he was into politics and elected. Alas that never materialised, if anything, Mike completely ignored him. Jack knew Mike didn't owe him anything, but Jack did help Mike construct his campaign leaflets and had been a good buddy to Mike just prior to Mike winning the safe seat in Kingston. Jack was not one for being too direct; he did not want to ask why Mike had not helped him into to work for Mike. Especially now Mike was flying high, Jack felt immensely let down. Mike chirped up, 'so what are you up to now?' 'I am unemployed as it happens and working on a novel, fiction.' 'Oh right, sorry to hear that' said Mike. Jack lost his job the year earlier due to cut backs at work. 'What are you here for?' said Mike. 'A new bow tie. I'm learning how to tie them' said Jack. 'Well I won't keep you long' said Jack. As he shook hands once more, turned and headed to the tie rack. Mike remarked 'all the best'. In addition, that was it. Jack knew that he was never going to become a politician; he had tried, numerous times. However, getting into the Conservative party and becoming a candidate is a mission. Typically, you need to have gone to Oxford or Cambridge Universities. Jack had been too average and lazy for that. Jack always wondered what it would have been like to be approved and selected as a candidate. In the end, resigning himself to a life as an average Joe, he continued to work in advertising in the vain hope of paying off bills and climbing the ladder so to speak. Mike finished his whisky and got up; he walked to the owner, shook hands and then turned to Steve and said 'let's go'. Back to Whitehall and his apartment there. Mike was like that, he could be selfish. I guess, he just figured, where was Jack's value. Mike was flying high now, had everything he wanted. When he got home he told his wife he bumped into an old friend. His wife said, 'and after all that, you didn't offer him a job? You tight fisted bastard. Here you have young people helping you, loyal, not speaking out. Someone you can trust and all you do is ignore him. Wow Mike Scott, you are shallow after all.' Mike turned and looked in the mirror, for the first time in a while, he actually felt guilty. This wasn't something Mike knew well, if anything, he rarely admitted fault for anything. He had a dinner at the Army and Navy club off Pall Mall scheduled for later in the week, he always loved this particular club. He felt at home here and rarely had to put up with the political drama of the other clubs like Whites, etc. The dinner was with Lord Irving, Lord Maguire and Lord Grey a former Chief of the Air Staff (CAS). The dinner was always a lively affair, a private room for the four of them. Starting with a few chasers, after already having had a few pints, wine was flowing at the table. The conversation flitted in and out between work and play. Often, the four of them still joked about the talent in the offices of Westminster. Despite being old enough to be their father, Mike often checked out the fillies as they paraded the grounds of Whitehall. He even found himself embroiled in the *#metoo* accusations that flew around with the various celebrity and political sex abuse scandals. Not that Mike gave a damn, quite the contrary; he had never put a foot wrong. Rather, he might have been a bit flirty whilst drunk. However, that was it. He still could not believe that he was slandered so badly a few years earlier. With Lord Irving laughing aloud as he too had a reputation as a bit of a player. Mrs Irving was well known to have seen first-hand the evidence against her husband, but knew full well, that given the nature of his job. She forgave him. 'Amber would have my balls' said Mike, if I had put a foot wrong. 'Variety is all I will say dear fellow.' Said Lord Irving. In addition, they continue in deep conversation, cracking jokes and drinking into the early hours. The waiting staff knew these four all too well and rolled their eyes at the prospect of having to help these four drunks into taxis come the end of the night. Despite the skin full, Mike always managed to drag himself out of bed in the morning. He had concluded that letting his hair down once a week with the lads was a good thing, regardless of the pressures of his job. He wanted to keep his marbles and knew that this bunch were the best company in all his years in politics. Ironic, that they were all former military types. The top of their field mind you. Mike had had a particularly heavy session because he knew the following day; the findings of the yearlong inquiry were going to be publicly announced. It was grim reading. Mike had seen the report the previous week before it came out and he knew about the deaths and casualties of the attacks. He knew many of the MPs who were gunned down or fatally wounded and to think that the final death total was two hundred and eight MPs. With four thousand six hundred and three civilians perishing. It was Britain's 9/11 without a shadow of a doubt. The government under Prime Minister Albrighton did not like the numbers and the Cabinet had done everything in their power to suppress the news. By releasing as much bad news as they could in the run up to the big day. But nothing could detract from the sheer scale of the atrocity. Ministers were trying to spend everything, from cost overruns of railway projects, the benefits system costing a fortune to the computer glitches at the NHS. The public weren't interested. They were quite simply still feeling raw from the attacks a year earlier. Public opinion was still in favour of the government response and leading figures like Mike actually had relatively high poll ratings. Which to most politicians is like gold dust. Mention a poll rating to a politician and typically they go into meltdown. Mike was doing the rounds at hospital. His good friend Stuart Williams MP was shot seven times and somehow managed to survive. A year later he was still receiving therapy for his wounds and Mike wanted to convey his support for Stuart. 'What are you doing here again Mike?' said Stuart Williams. 'Here for you, you plonker.' 'Well, you know how I feel about visitors, I would much rather you left me alone.' Said Stuart. 'Tough' replied Mike. 'Until you are up and running again, you can expect to see me on a regular basis.' St Thomas' hospital opposite Westminster was at the forefront of receiving casualties during the attacks. With the A&E department totally overwhelmed due to the scale of patient numbers. A new building project was now underway, knocking down the old building and re-building on the open space. It was like using one space for the other and the foundations had just gone in. It would take another year before the new hospital wing at St Thomas' would be up, but still Mike wasn't happy. He was not health secretary, but he made sure every time he visited the wounded, he made a 'b' line for the Chief Executive of the Trust. Chasing him along to push for an earlier construction timetable.

Despite the sheer scale of the mess the UK found itself in and all the terrorist related activity. The Russians were not being helpful. With record numbers of Russians operatives working out of their Embassy in Notting Hill to the frequent incursions by Russian heavy bombers into UK airspace. Each time the QRA or quick reaction alert squadron of the RAF was scrambled. Consisting of nine aircraft, Mike knew that this was never going to be enough. So, he ordered an additional squadron of Eurofighter Typhoon interceptors also consisting of nine aircraft be stood to. Meaning that the UK had in Scotland eighteen aircraft on standby bringing the UK up to nearly twenty percent of cold war levels. One of the problems Mike had also identified was that each time fighters were launched to police air space, Voyager AirTankers were regularly required for air to air refuelling. The problem was that these aircraft were based down in Oxfordshire at Brize Norton. Some hour or more away from RAF Lossiemouth. Mike ordered that four of this fleet be transferred to Scotland to cut down the flying time to refuelling. It caused a bit of a stir within the RAF, but the reality was that this made perfect sense. Mike also ordered double the number of Typhoon aircraft to be based out of RAF *Northolt* in London for cover for the Capital. He also wanted double the number of Apache aircraft on standby for London as they were invaluable during the original attacks. They were now common sight, as they regularly patrolled London airspace, winding up and down the River Thames. All of this was coming at a cost and the Treasury were making a lot of noises behind the scenes. Mike just walked into Harry Albrighton and said, 'I propose we increase defence spending to five percent of GDP.' 'You what?' said Albrighton. 'Yes, five per cent. If we don't we won't be able to adequately prepare and prevent similar attacks in future' said Mike. Albrighton trusted Mike implicitly and said 'leave it with me'. Mike was never one to beat about the bush. 'On the topic of defence, I have ordered a QRA evaluation with orders for two Typhoon aircraft to fly over Westminster from Northolt, based on a real-life exercise situation. If you come with me into the rose garden, they should appear in about thirty seconds.' Together, Mike and Harry walked out briskly to the garden at the rear of Downing Street and there it was in the sky, two RAF Typhoon aircraft flew over, with their EJ2000 engines roaring into the distance. Mike got onto his mobile phone and called RAF Command, 'have the fighters circle Westminster for a couple of minutes then return to base'. 'Roger that' replied the RAF Command officer. Mike turned to the PM and said 'quite simply, we believe our email communications may have been hacked and I am proposing we start to use secure courier once more to minimise leaks.' 'Ah right, that would explain it. But was not secure courier used a couple of decades ago?' said Albrighton. 'Yes. But it works well.' Said Mike. 'We have to cut the number of leaks as best as possible and we believe it is the Russians who are up to no good' said Mike. 'How on earth did they manage to hack our encrypted email system?' said the PM. 'We are still working on that.' Replied Mike. 'Ok Mike I will leave that with you, let me know how you get on. I have got to go to a press conference now and take more questions about the Inquiry.' Albrighton turned at speed and proceeded through to the press meeting room at Downing Street. Before entering, he saw his head speech writer who handed him a freshly printed copy of the speech he was about to deliver. As Albrighton stood before the lectern, he began by playing with his hair. He often did, it was his signature. 'Today ladies and gentlemen, I am here to take more questions from the press on the nature of the attacks and to answer as best as possible those questions that remain unanswered.' The assembled media pack was buzzing, they had an abundance of questions outstanding from Albrighton's announcement in the temporary house of commons in the QE centre in Westminster. 'Prime Minister, Prime Minister' said an eager *DBC news* Chief Political Correspondent. 'Is it true that former Prime Minister Matthews knew about the impending attacks, the threat levels and still wanted to press ahead with cuts to the armed forces and security services?' 'In answer to your question, I think it is important that we look forward not backwards. But yes, that is true.' A rumble took hold of the press pack, the correspondents all began to talk to one another and the noise in the meeting room actually became quite loud. Albrighton immediately realised this and said 'next question, John Alexander from *ETV* please' and the press conference continued at a pace. It left the viewing public much clearer on what government had been up to. But the response to the cuts was what got the public the most angry. Crowds gathered outside Downing Street protesting about cuts to the military. Some three hundred people had marched from Parliament Square to Downing Street. Whilst three hundred was not a big number, it nevertheless was unprecedented in that, very rarely did the public ever complain about the state of the military. Now Albrighton had a crowd on his doorstep. Albrighton ordered his head of research to conduct a number of polls from different polling companies to assess the public mood towards the military. He found that an overwhelming ninety-one per cent of the public supported the armed forces with an additional eighty-two per cent calling for cuts to be reversed. It was all Albrighton needed. He was going off public opinion, something that Mike hated doing. To Mike political decisions should be taken for the good of the nation, regardless of public opinion. Albrighton however was a betting man, he hadn't got to number ten by chance. He knew that this polling data would give him the ammunition to argue within cabinet the need to increase defence spending to five per cent of GDP. And indeed he did, he got about it right away, calling an urgent Cabinet meeting on the matter, which was approved after much toing and froing. Most politicians tended to be quite spineless and opinion less, unless they had a script or were pre-prepared to say something, very few of them actually had an opinion. This suited people like Mike who did have opinions and he was not afraid to air them.

Mike wanted the British public to see first-hand that he as Defence Secretary was taking their security seriously. So, he set about placing an order for the infantry for five thousand M60 heavy machine guns from the Americans, with bipods, sights, straps, and plenty of ammunition. The US Navy sent the weapons via heavy lift freighter by sea to Plymouth harbour. Mike ordered the Army to receive them upon arrival in port and distribute them to the various infantry units across the country for training and development. He also ordered one hundred of them be sent to Sandhurst military academy. He decided he himself would be the first to test fire the weapon on the firing range. He had his press team organise the media and he had them all meet him at Sandhurst in early September. Mike wearing military fatigues, marched out to the firing range where the assembled press pack waited for him. He gave a brief speech about how the US and the UK were strengthening ties and this weapons deal demonstrated that. Mike then proceeded with the aid of a weapons technician to fire the M60 for the first time. Aiming through the sights, he gripped the handle, holding down the weapon with his left hand. He then gently squeezed the trigger, to his surprise the weapon fired a huge burst of rounds. And boy did it roar. Mike ceased fire, but how he loved it. He turned to the photographers and cameramen and smiled. He then turned back to the target and fired again. For the lay person this might be a simple exercise, but to Mike this demonstrated the awesome firepower the UK had just acquired for its infantry. When used effectively, the M60 would represent a new change of direction for the British military, not only was Mike committed to equipping them as well as possible. He wanted to capitalise on the media war and use psychological influences to make would be terrorists think twice.

Speaking of change of direction, the Russians were really beginning to piss off Mike. Aside from the suspected email hack, the airspace incursions and the numerous operatives running about. Mike was too busy to have to keep checking up on this lot. So, he arranged a meeting with the Russian Ambassador to London. Mike wanted better terms with Russia. It was obvious that Russia would not stop this activity. But Mike a peaceful man at heart wanted to start a new process of engagement with Russia. So, come early October, Mike arranged for the Ambassador to come and visit him at his office on Whitehall. It was unprecedented. Surprisingly this did not leak. The Russians took this kind of thing very seriously and wanted to first see how the meeting went before deciding to leak its contents. That was how they worked. 'Good morning Comrade Ambassador' said Mike with a grin on his face. 'Good morning Defence Secretary.' Ambassador Duslov said back. 'First time on Whitehall? Can I get you tea or coffee?' replied Mike. 'Tea, please, white, no sugar' Mike pressed on his intercom, 'Amanda, two teas please, no sugar.' 'Yes Sir' replied Amanda, Mike's secretary. 'Where can I begin, Mr Ambassador, let me express my delight in you attending today. I am very pleased we should have the opportunity to speak in person. That way you can hopefully convey the sincerity of my remarks to your superiors.' Said Mike. 'I personally thank you on behalf of the Russian Federation for your hospitality and extension of goodwill to discuss important matters.' Duslov's accent was clear, he had been educated at Oxford, but still his Russian pronunciation came through. Despite the slight age gap, Mike was fifteen years his senior, Duslov was long suspected of being the Head of the GRU and FSB in Britain. So, to Mike this was indeed important. Mike had hoped his light-hearted joke about calling him 'comrade' would go down well. It appeared to have worked. Duslov sat back in his chair and pushed the glasses on his nose further up. 'You see, my government has many issues with the UK. First off we firmly dislike the aggression of the Royal Navy submarines encroaching on Russian naval bases.' Despite the reduced number of boats, the Royal Navy had indeed been in Russian waters placing much of the Russian fleet under surveillance along with regular satellite coverage, the Royal Navy was able to pick up a fairly good picture on Russian naval capabilities. Which had been renewed from the Soviet era. Mike however, wanted the Royal Navy to increase the size of the submarine fleet, increasing the number of Astute class submarines from seven to fifteen. Mike leaned forward placing his arms on his desk, 'you mean to tell me that the Royal Navy has been operating in Russian waters? Why I will investigate this immediately.' Mike quipped. 'Why, Mr Secretary, please spare me the pleasantries, we know you know about this already.' Mike sat back, took a breath and said 'Why yes, indeed, you are right.' It was again unprecedented for a British minister to accept the accusation of a Russian Ambassador, particularly in light of the deteriorating relations. 'Well, seeing that we are being blunt, I will reply in kind. Your aircraft are regularly encroaching on UK airspace which we find totally unacceptable.' Said Mike. 'However, rather than escalate things further, can I propose that we both stop this petty activity and start afresh? I will call off UK submarines from Russian waters if you stop the heavy bombers.' Said Mike. 'Naturally, I cannot speak for my leadership; however, I will convey this message with the utmost urgency.' Said Duslov. 'Let us consider this a new beginning of UK/ Russia relations' said Mike. 'If we can make this work, then there is no reason why we cannot have further meetings to discuss progress on other issues?' with that Duslov smiled and nodded. It was a strange meeting in that, Duslov had shown respect for his elder statesman and Mike had equally shown respect via the honesty with which he was willing to tolerate. Amanda walked in with a tray carrying two teas, as she placed them down on the table, the Ambassador stood up. 'No thank you' he said, 'I must go now'. He stood, extended his hand to Mike, shook hands, then promptly turned and walked out. 'Please show the Ambassador out.' Mike said to Amanda. 'Very good Sir.' She replied. Mike leant back in his chair and thought to himself about what had just happened. A lightning visit by a Russian Ambassador, in which, he had personally negotiated about removing the air threat to UK PLC by giving up British submarine presence in Russian waters. It seemed a good deal. Whether the Russians would go for it would be another thing. But the reality was that Mike needed good news to placate the Cabinet who were uneasy at Mike's approach towards National Security. Mike wanted to demonstrate he had the power to make things happen, with or without the Cabinet. Just as the Ambassador put on his grey mac, standing near the door, Mike said, 'I have another very small matter of a certain Jack Cakebread, we believe he was put under surveillance by Russia and China, we'd like that to stop please.' The Ambassador turned his head and said, 'why Mr Secretary, I will relay your request to my superiors' and promptly left the building. A week went by without reply from the Russians. There were no leaks, no mention of any meetings in the press. All was quiet. Then suddenly out of the blue, a message was sent by email to Mike's office from the Russian Ambassador. In it he requested to return the hospitality of the previous week at the Russian residence in Kensington. Naturally, Mike didn't want to appear too eager, but at the same time didn't want to be rude. So, he replied about an hour after initially reading the email, accepting the invite for a week later. Mike went to the Russian residence with his usual escort. Upon arrival, he and his team were invited inside. Mike spotted his old massage parlour (above board) at Notting Hill Gate, 'I must remember to book a massage' he said to himself. Back at the Russian Ambassador's residence, Mike was ushered through to the private office of the Ambassador. He was early, so the secretary, who received Mike, invited him to sit in the office and wait. As he did, he could not help but look around. The incredible wood panelling of the Russian interior was notable; it was darkened wood and had the feel of something out of a haunted house. Mike wandered around the office, looking first at the paintings on the wall, then the photos that adorned Duslov's desk. A portrait of Vladimir Pushkin adored the wall behind his seat. Mike then decided to sit down facing it. He waited, fifteen minutes past their original meeting time and was just about to get up and leave, when the Ambassador came rushing in. 'I am terribly sorry for the delay Mr Secretary, I was just on the phone with the President.' Mike looked pleased and soon forgot that he had been kept waiting. 'That is good news' said Mike. 'We want to get things moving.' Said Mike. 'Ok so, the President has said, he is willing to stop all air incursions and for that matter submarine incursions by Russia into UK territorial space. In exchange you will stop your submarines, redirect your satellites elsewhere and stop any RAF surveillance flights near Russian airspace.' Said Duslov. 'Well, it is good to hear that we have some movement at last. I will agree to stopping the subs, then I will look at the satellite issue. I cannot guarantee anything just yet.' Said Mike. 'Ok let us work this out properly, we want you to stop all surveillance of Russian assets, including via GCHQ.' Duslov exclaimed. 'That is out of the question, we survey you just as you survey us. I will stop the subs, and redirect the satellites, but I cannot stop GCHQ.' 'Please forgive me, my manners, can I offer you a drink?' said Duslov. 'Cognac would be nice please.' Said Mike. Duslov spoke in Russian to his staff via the phone on his desk. Instantly, a man appeared with a drink on the tray, it was cognac, the finest from France. Mike thanked him and picked up the glass, took a sip and smiled. 'Very good' he said. 'Only the best' said Duslov. 'Now, we have agreement on this?' said Duslov. 'Yes' replied Mike. 'I shall convey this message to our President, who I am sure will be very happy.' Mike nodded. 'We are not at war with you' said Mike. 'Quite the contrary, we seek new ways of working with you, but there are still many obstacles, especially politically speaking. Westminster MPs would jump on this if they knew we were talking.' Said Mike. 'Steps have been taken to minimise any leaks should we say.' Duslov smiled. Mike felt that he was on the same wavelength as Duslov, despite the age difference; Mike felt that he was someone the UK could do business with. 'I shall have to go now' said Mike, putting the empty glass down. 'Perhaps the next time we meet, we can have lunch?' said Mike. 'Good suggestion.' Said Duslov. With that, Mike stood and walked to the door. Duslov escorted him personally to his Land Rover. They shook hands and Mike was whisked off back to Whitehall where he set about redirecting all submarines and satellites. He also ordered that all passcodes be changed every month. His fear was that these may indeed be compromised and the last thing he wanted was an unauthorised launch of weapons or a compromise of communications. He went over to number ten and explained to Albrighton what he had planned to do and that he was keeping to it. Albrighton, agreed, surprisingly. He appeared to be distracted by something and Mike wondered why this was all approved so quickly. It turned out that Albrighton had been having an affair with a page three girl and news was about to break to the public. It wasn't a problem as Albrighton was already divorced and living the life of riley. 'Fancy a game of whiff whaff?' said Albrighton to Mike. 'You what?' said Mike. 'Ping Pong, you know?' said Albrighton and with that Mike found himself, playing table tennis in the back yard of number ten with the Prime Minister. Albrighton really loved his table tennis and it was beginning to grow on Mike, but reality was he had a thousand and one things to be getting on with. It entertained the PM and that was important enough for Mike. 'I have decided to cut back the *DBC* and privatise it.' Said Albrighton. We are going for full privatisation and IPO listing next year on the London Stock Exchange. I told them that we could no longer continue to subsidise the opposition mouth piece. I also told the Secretary of State for Culture, Media and Sport that we would be privatising *Channel Four* as well' said Albrighton. 'I bet that went down well' said Mike. 'Like a lead weight. But you know what, I don't give a fuck. They have been bloody awkward since I took over, in fact,, they've always been bloody awkward. So now is the time to raise some money for the Treasury, keep them happy, and sell off *DBC* and *Channel Four*.' Albrighton smashed the ball down winning the point. Mike picked the ball up off the grass. 'Anything else you want to do? I mean, a legacy is important, the last thing you want is to work on that in your final year, you should be working on that now.' Said Mike. 'Come to think of it, we are going to re-introduce subsidies for private health care, introduce a ten-pound charge for visiting your GP and A&E.' Albrighton exclaimed, slapping the ball wide of the table. 'I think that sounds reasonable' said Mike. 'Well, you see, we can't have drunks abusing A&E all the time, charging them to use it will soon stop that. Same with GPs, they have long complained they are over worked. So, I figured let's start charging and put a value on the NHS. We can no longer afford to be free.' Albrighton said. 'How do you think this will go down?' 'Also like a lead balloon. But it has to be done, so I am pressing ahead with these reforms.'

Albrighton continued, 'you recall my plans for a new Thames Estuary Airport? Well, that is back on again, except I have managed to get the entire project privately financed from the Americans of all, can you believe it? They often complained about the Chinese building our nuclear reactors. So, I thought, why not use my American roots and get the begging bowl out. You would be surprised how generous they were and being American, want the biggest and best money can buy. Even their current President Donald Masterson has agreed to help get the private investors on board. It's nothing short of a miracle.' Said Albrighton. Mike leant forward and picked the ball out of the net. Started by serving once more. 'That's good news, any chance you can get them to invest in some of our other big infrastructure projects like Crossrail or even the new Hospital rebuilds?' said Mike. 'I thought you didn't care about that kind of thing Mike?' said Albrighton. 'Well since the attacks, rebuilding and renewing Britain is all I can think of.' With that, Albrighton stopped. He looked up at Mike and said 'you know what, you are right. Let's make this a much larger initiative and put the focus on the renewal after the terror attacks.' Mike wasn't short of being amazed, particularly because Albrighton used to be such a thought-out fellow, in that he always went by polling data. Which, in this instance had shown the public against private investments like this.

'You know one thing Bashir hasn't done?' said Mike. 'What is that?' said Albrighton. 'He hasn't increased the number of armed police since the attacks. I suspect we cannot keep troops on the streets indefinitely, so we will have to look to increase the number of armed officers and ARVs across the country by two hundred per cent. If not consider arming ALL officers.' Said Mike. Albrighton looked at him and smiled. 'You know Mike, you are always on the button, most of that lot in Cabinet haven't done a bloody thing since the attacks except complain. Here, on the other hand you have been busy all over the place, single handed making more of an impact that most put together.' Said Albrighton. 'Why thank you Harry.' Mike said, also smiling back at Albrighton.

'With Brexit just having been completed, we are set for some pretty good growth in terms of GDP' said Albrighton. 'I would like you to have a look at the numbers and let me know what you think?' 'Why certainly' said Mike. 'Oh, and I would like to have a go on one of those Fast Jets, do you think you could arrange that?' said Albrighton. 'Why not, but bring your sick bag' said Mike.

Meanwhile in the South Atlantic, tensions were brewing once more as Argentina sent four Chinese made Chengdu J10 aircraft over Falkland Island Airspace. This alarmed Mike. For he knew that the Royal Navy was half the size it was when compared to the last war. Despite ordering thirty Type 26 Frigates, only four had been delivered and the fleet was in a state of flux with the Type 23s pretty much worn out and being placed in reserve. It would take a colossal effort to re-equip the Royal Navy. Given that the RAF only had four interceptors based out of the Falklands, Mike immediately ordered nine more aircraft be dispatched to bolster air policing in the islands. He also ordered the immediate movement of three extra regular army battalions to be permanently stationed there, with heavy armour, artillery and ground-based air defence weapons in the form of Sky Sabre and Star Streak respectively. Mike ensured that ten of the systems were deployed to the Falklands permanently. He also ordered regular patrols by the Astute class fleet, redirecting them from Russian waters to the South Atlantic. China was not happy with the UK sailing through their territorial waters in the Far East with Royal Navy ships. In direct opposition, they openly threatened to re-arm the entire Argentine military with the very latest brand-new equipment. From helicopters, tanks, fast jets and light weapons. Mike wanted to make a week-long visit to the Falklands to ensure preparations were underway to prevent any such aggression. It was indeed a case of to declare peace you need to prepare for war. Mike called the PM from his satellite phone on the Voyager transport as it took off from Sao Paolo in Brazil. 'Hello Harry, can you hear me?' said Mike. 'Clear as anything Mike. Go ahead' said Albrighton. 'I am nearly in the Falklands, suggest you let the press know so we can use the media attention to strengthen our position internationally. We also want to invite the US Navy here on a training exercise. They had said they would avoid the region to remain neutral, but now we really need one of their carrier battle groups down here as a show of strength. Our carrier battle group is still being constructed and it will be some years yet before we would be able to show any presence down here.' Said Mike. 'Well let me get on the phone to Donald Masterson's office and see what we can organise. He may not be able to send an entire task force, but perhaps one or two ships?' Albrighton confirmed. 'That's better than nothing' said Mike. 'I will give you another update once I have had time to assess things on the ground, Mike out.'

'I have just had an idea also, lets invite the Brazilian Navy to visit the Falklands' said Mike. 'Are you trying to provoke or placate the Argentines' said his chief of staff. 'Good point.' 'We will continue to work with the Brazilians to maintain our air transport links, and nothing more at this time. I just hope we aren't too late.' Mike's plane landed on schedule, it was the middle of the night and he was met by an Army land rover that picked him up and took him straight to the Command centre. Upon arrival he was briefed by the assembled military personnel and took a look at the latest satellite imagery of large numbers of Argentine troops on manoeuvres south of Buenos Aires.

'One thing is for sure this time round, we are not going to get caught with our trousers down. I have already ordered the three services to bolster their permanent presence here. More funds will be allocated in due course and we will look to increase where necessary our defences. I have asked Lord Irving to conduct a full assessment and he is working on that as we speak. Lord Irving's ship HMS *Agamemnon* was sunk off Falkland sound during the last conflict so he has first-hand knowledge of the area.' Said Mike, he went on 'let me be clear gentlemen, my objective and orders are as follows: prepare for war to secure peace. I do not want a conflict here. Now let's get to work.' Mike went off to the mess room and had a full English fry up. One thing he loved more than anything was bacon and liver, the commanding officer of the Falklands garrison, a certain Lieutenant General Nash made sure Mike got that at the very least. Once fed and watered, Mike's entourage began their day by having an aerial tour of the main, anticipated landing grounds. They were all mined and British artillery had them in full range, so anything landing here would be completely obliterated. 'I want it blatantly obvious to the Argies from their reconnaissance that making a landing would be suicide.' Said Mike. 'With heavy armour arriving within the next two weeks, this would make any ground assault very difficult. But be under no illusion, if they do have the latest weapons from the Chinese, this would be a very bloody battle.' Once they landed back at the main airbase, Mike wanted to go out by Jeep and visit many of the vantage points. He wanted to see first-hand the possible sites for the ground-based Sky Sabre systems. He wanted total air defence cover from these systems to complement the RAF Typhoons. This would make it very difficult for the Argentine Air Force to penetrate Falkland airspace. 'Everything will be here in a matter of weeks, I sound like I am repeating myself, but the reality is these things take time to move. The one thing we are short on is Royal Navy ships. I have ordered HMS *Westminster* here, she is *en route* now, accompanied by HMS *Astute*. Once Astute arrives, I want to make it abundantly clear to the Argies that we have a boat in the region. Have her sit outside Punta Alta port, outside of their Exclusive Economic Zone (EEZ), northwest of us here.' The adrenaline was flowing in Mike. He was getting on a bit, but none of this phased him one bit. He wanted to make sure he prevented a conflict from ever happening by ensuring that he had overwhelming force available. 'Punta Alta is their main naval base. Although I suspect, if they were to consider an amphibious landing they may use Rio Gallegos, or somewhere further south from their main naval base. Either way, this is a defensive action, we are not going to bomb their air fields or ports at this time, it is too risky. We will focus on the core protection of the Islands instead.' It all felt a million miles away from London. With all this military activity buzzing around, Mike had totally forgot about his main responsibility of protecting the UK mainland. 'Have RFA *Wave Ruler* head down here to the Falklands, I want her here on standby.' Mike said to his accompanying Admiral. 'She was due to be sold to Brazil sir' 'well not any more, have that bloody ship sent down here on the double. Apologise to the Brazilians and offer them the prospect of us building them a new refueller from Camel Laird.'

Mike finished his tour of the main vantage points and headed back to the main barracks. From there he called the PM again on his satellite phone, playing with the antenna, he extended it and then dialled the number. 'Harry it's me, listen, we need to get things moving quick sharp if we are going to avoid another war down here.' Said Mike. 'OK, well Mike, the cabinet doesn't feel the need to move so quickly, if anything they feel you are being far too hasty.' Albrighton exclaimed. 'Well, I disagree with you, and I have already ordered various assets into position, until such time that we can be clear that there is no threat.' 'OK Mike, your call, and for the record, you are in charge of Defence. I will leave that to you.' 'Quite right' said Mike as he hung up on the PM. Mike wasn't happy, but he was equally unhappy of a repeat of 1982. 'The orders stand, carry on Lieutenant General' said Mike. Mike was on the Islands for a week and wanted to visit everything, and inspect all parts of the islands. The main build up of forces had in fact caused an international incident with Argentina calling for the UK to restrain itself and avoid another conflict. Mike was furious, to him, this was nothing more than sensible precautions designed to prevent any escalation. Mike turned on *Global News* and the headlines were quite stark, 'Argentina declares Falklands theirs'. Mike was indeed worried, with the media now stirring up things, he knew time was of the essence. He got on the phone to the Admiralty and ordered them to move at full speed when sailing the equipment down to the Falklands. The islands now had some three thousand regular army troops stationed there and would soon have one hundred main battle tanks, three hundred warrior infantry fighting vehicles and two hundred extra jeeps.

In Buenos Aires the crowds drew larger and larger by the day, protesting against the UK occupation of the Malvinas or Falklands. Protestors gathered outside the British Embassy, but where beaten back by riot police who were there is great numbers. Only a couple of years earlier the then Chancellor of the UK visited Argentina on a trade mission, designed to ease tensions. To some hardliners in the UK, this was seen as a move by a weak Chancellor to buy off Argentina from ever attacking the Falklands as it would be the cheaper option. In terms of the cost of paying for Defence, the UK had shirked its responsibilities for some time and the former Chancellor was well known for his cuts, ironically calling for 'Singapore on Thames' with regard to a post Brexit Britain, but that is an aside.. But this had now changed under new British leadership, Mike had all the funds he needed and was taking charge of the entire situation. With vast quantities of Oil recently discovered within Falkland waters, let alone the rich fishing grounds. The UK was not about to give up this territory lightly, if anything they would put up a fight to defend it. Mike's week drew to a close and he climbed the stairs on to his waiting Voyager for the long trip back to London. Just before he took off, Mike called the PM again, this time asking that the Foreign Secretary be dispatched to Argentina for talks on preventing the crises from escalating further. The PM unfortunately refused, saying that there was no crisis and that the Foreign Secretary was needed in Japan for a trade mission. Mike began to realise that perhaps he was on his own on this one, but nevertheless, this was something he was accustomed to. Whilst in Bosnia, he was the UN Commander and sole in charge of military activity there. On more than one occasion, he had to make decisions often without consulting higher authority. Like when he discovered that local Muslims were being shelled by the Bosnian Serb nationalist forces, Mike decided to move his Warrior vehicles into position next to houses and buildings, so that if they were hit by the incoming fire. Mike would use that as an act of provocation and order his men to return fire. Mike was not afraid of firing back. Mike had flash backs though, something that he did not admit to people. On more than one occasion Mike would stand and stare out the window as he recalled the explosions and gun fire that rang out. Fortunately for him, time was a healer and he began more and more to become used to this as the years wore on. But the sight of dead bodies still haunted him and he sometimes had difficulty sleeping at night, tossing and turning. The sudden jolt of the Voyager as it hit a pocket of turbulence, hit Mike. He jumped in his seat. Then realising where he was, rolled over and tried to go back to sleep again. The pilot had just come over the intercom to say that they were two hours from landing and that breakfast would soon be served. Mike could smell the bacon from the galley, and that brought him round. Sitting upright in his seat, Mike lowered the tray table and waited for his breakfast to be served to him. The flight was empty so this would not take long, the Voyager jolted again as the turbulence hit once more and the fasten seat belt signs suddenly appeared on. Food was then placed down on his tray table and Mike began to tuck in. After eating, he walked up to the washroom to freshen up and then proceeded onto the cockpit to thank the crew. He did not have time to hang about when the plane landed, so wanted to get thankyous out of the way prior to landing. 'How does she fly?' Mike asked the Captain. 'Relatively well, although the engines feel like they lack power at times. We also do not have counter measures or long-range radar. Whoever signed the deal for these aircraft didn't think we would need them.' Mike rolled his eyes as usual and replied 'we will see what we can do about that'. With that, he turned and walked out of the cockpit and back to his seat for landing. Upon arrival at London Heathrow, he briskly got off the plane and into his awaiting Land Rover. Lights flashing from the escort out riders, he was driven at speed to Whitehall. The time was approximately eight in the morning. Traffic would be busy on the route into London. Mike asked where his helicopter was and was surprised to hear that it was in deep maintenance and had not be certified to fly yet. Hence why they were taking the road. Mike wasn't happy about the lack of helicopter availability.

Mike had just walked into the situation room at the MoD building on Whitehall when an aide came rushing in. 'Sir' said the young Lieutenant. 'We have just received notification that six Argentine aircraft were reported to have entered Falkland Island airspace and were subsequently chased off by the QRA teams.' He continued 'no reports of any other activity yet. How shall we proceed?' 'Carry on, tell the base commander the following: continue to exercise caution, protect EEZ and Territorial air space. Report back if breached.' That was it, Mike wanted to keep it simple for the time being. Mike had bags under his eyes, the flight back was long and tiring and he didn't really manage to sleep. He knew that the cabinet were meeting later that day and that the wolves would be at him for taking on this crises single handed. As he walked across the road from the MoD building to Number Ten Downing Street, he came across a group of protestors, also ironically complaining about the Falklands Islands 'occupation'. They were trade union members, anti-war protestors and generally random types who had nothing better to do. They numbered around fifty. The screech of the loud haler annoyed Mike. It was loud and unnecessary he thought. His security team were close by and they all continued on through the main gates of Downing Street. Once inside, the Cabinet were all assembled, the room was stuffy, felt almost like a tube carriage on a busy morning. Mike took his seat next to the Environment Secretary on his left and his good friend Esther McCarthy on his right, Secretary of State for Work and Pensions. The meeting began with the usual update from the PM on the state of the economy, he was really chuffed as GDP had just been revised up by 0.2 percentage points to 0.7 per cent growth for the previous quarter. 'I want you all promoting the economy' said Albrighton, 'I want you to provide me with names who wants to speak on TV this next 48 hours? Ok seeing that no one has replied I will chose ten of you. Mike you good to speak?' Mike was taken unawares, still a little jaded from his long flight, Mike nodded in agreement. The PM reeled off the nine other names and said everyone was to stand up for the economy and promote it at every opportunity. The meeting seemed to go on for an age. With the PM prattling on about this and that, campaign issues, the forthcoming party conference, you name it. Mike just sat there in his chair, leaning back and waiting to be asked for an update. But strangely, this never happened. The PM called a close to the meeting and that was that. Mike looked at Albrighton and said 'don't you want to hear about what I have been up to this past week?' 'No, not really, we will keep it open until our next cabinet session.' And with that Albrighton got up and walked straight out the room. Esther turned and whispered to Mike 'don't worry about it'.

Intelligence was a vital matter for Mike, he wanted to know more about what was going on in Argentina and he wanted regular updates on the Kalahari operations and the domestic terror front. So he set about holding regular meetings with the head of MI6, and his top ten agents. All were invited into to London and the MoD building on Whitehall. It was a little like Piccadilly Circus at times. One after the other the agents entered the building nine men and one woman. As Mike walked through to the meeting room where they were all assembled, he bumped into one of the agents in the corridor. A youngish man around forty to forty five years old. Mike wanted to hear directly from those on the front line who were in the thick of it. This was slightly different to regular protocol. He had had previous meetings with top agents one on one, but rarely so many in the same room at the same time. 'Minister, I must protest at the nature of this meeting. It is highly unusual to have so many key operatives in the same place at the same time.' Said the Head of MI6, C. 'Understood and noted. I also remember the helicopter crash on the Mull of Kintyre that took out the heads of MI6, MI5, GCHQ and local police from Northern Ireland. It was a terrible crash. One that I have never forgotten. It happened under

John Minors government, and he strenuously denied any foul play. When you look back at it now, you can't help but think perhaps it might have been. But that case is closed and not why we are here today.' Mike finished. C chipped in and said 'can I politely suggest that we rotate attendees so as to avoid us all being in the same place at the same time?' 'Agreed' said Mike and that was the conclusion of the matter. C's face lit up and was clearly quite happy at the result. He knew Mike could be difficult when he wanted to, but even to him this was important not to mess up. Mike reminded 'C' that immediately after the 9/11 attacks, the heads of MI6, MI5 and GCHQ all flew on the 'same plane' to America. Mike said he did not want to see that happen ever again, 'we couldn't afford to lose you all at once' he said. 'If we don't have enough planes, buy more' he finished.

Upon leaving the meeting, Mike walked back into his office and issued a new directive in the form of ensuring that all helicopters had well maintained engines and where the engines were old, they should be replaced at speed. 'Pickering, come in here' said Mike. 'Take this order and get it out to the base commanders and head of maintenance. Make sure they acknowledge'. 'Roger that sir'. Said Pickering. Mike had monitored over the nineties and early two thousand the number of Royal Navy Lynx helicopters that had dropped out of the sky due to poor maintenance (check it out online). Mike didn't want that to happen on his watch and allocated extra funds to ensuring that this would not happen. 'Pickering, get me Rolls Royce on the phone' said Mike. 'Roger that Sir' said Pickering, handing him the handset. 'Hello, is that Mark Wallace, CEO?' Said Mike. 'Yes' replied Wallace. 'I need you to replace all our old helicopter engines and provide all the updated spare parts. Can you do it?' To Mike the matter was simple, but in reality, it was a technical situation. Lots of logistics and costs involved, but Irving knew how to keep ministers happy and just said 'Yes, we can do it'. With that Mike hung up and looked out his window onto Whitehall. Since the House of Commons was being rebuilt and Portcullis House likewise, Mike had to find new places to eat for lunch. So he headed out to Piccadilly with his escort. He had agreed to meet with Lord Irving for a bite at Franco's on Jermyn Street. Together they sat down and got slightly drunk on some very good French red wine. Discussing the goings on of the Westminster elite and the impending crises affecting the Falklands. 'You do realise Wilton's is next door?' Said Irving. 'Yes, I know that, but I thought Francos would do the trick for a change. With Westminster a construction site, I wanted to make the most of fine dining in town.' Said Mike. 'Well, the next one is on me, I can't have you expensing this all the time Mike. I owe you lunch at some point. How about next week Tuesday? I will find us somewhere swanky.' Said Irving. 'Fine, if you insist, but to be honest I hear Criterion is good this time of year.' Replied Mike. 'But I can't do Nobu unfortunately, with that actor De Rossi the owner, he's politically connected, we can't be seen there.' Chipped in Irving. 'Ok sure, I had never heard of it anyway.' Said Mike. 'Fancy a drink after? Duke's hotel is just round the corner and they do fantastic vodka martinis, let's go down for one' said Irving. 'Sure' replied Mike. As they paid up and made their way to Dukes, they sat down in the ornate lounge and marvelled at the bar, sparkling with all its finery. They ordered a couple of martinis and three or four later they found themselves drunkenly getting ready to leave. A small mouse ran across the floor in the distance near the kitchen door, Mike pointed it out and laughed. 'Perhaps he's got a better idea' said Mike in reference to what to do next on the Falklands and getting Westminster MPs support. Mike's Land Rover was waiting for him outside the hotel. Mike clambered aboard and headed back to his flat off the Mall. It was now early evening and Mike had had one too many to be of any use back in the office. It was but a stone's throw away from this particular watering hole, Mike had wanted to walk back, but his security team insisted on him using the Land Rover. The last thing they wanted was him falling over and giving himself a black eye. The security team however, did find it amusing, because Mike was one of the few ministers around who regularly got drunk. He and Lord Irving were well known for it and their reputations grew as a result, particularly with the military.

Come the next day Mike had a hang over, but remarkably, he was sprightly. Up and about eating his favourite bacon and liver first thing. He got on the phone to Pickering one of his aides at the MoD 'Pickering, are you there? Get me the latest report on the SA80 replacement. I want that on my desk when I get in.' 'Roger that sir.' Pickering ever the efficient bureaucrat come soldier or perhaps It was soldier come bureaucrat. Mike could never decide. But what he did know was that this young man was indeed valuable and helpful, moreover, knew how to keep his mouth shut. Something invaluable around Westminster. Mike's car pulled up for the short trip from his apartment to Whitehall. On the way there he looked up at Nelson's column and admired the grandeur of the statue. 'Not like that anymore' said Mike to his driver Mick Leadbetter. 'No sir.' Most of Mike's staff knew to keep conversations short and to the point. As the car drove down Whitehall they came up to the MoD building and Mike jumped out. Making his way up through to his office, which was adorned with paintings of various Army regiments and insignias. Portraits of famous generals of wars past. Mike sat down at his desk and saw the report sitting there ready for him to digest. He began to read it and spent a good thirty minutes going through, making notes on different pages, with a highlighter underlining specific points. To Mike getting rid of the SA80 rifle was imperative. During his time in the Army, the SA80 had jammed and regularly did not work. Mike knew that any modern fighting force needed a weapon that would work come rain, snow or sunny weather. 'Pickering get in here.' Mike said over his intercom. 'Right, take these notes and get them off to procurement, copy in the head of the Army and weapons training. The note began 'it is my recommendation that we get rid of the SA80 asap and replace it with a rifle like the AK47. Something that works no matter what the conditions. So I am interested in hearing more about the AR-15, H&K 416 and the M4, but by all means, if you know of a better replacement, then speak up. I want a live weapons demonstration next week Thursday.' With that Mike pointed to the door and Pickering left. Mike had a speech to make in the House of Lords, or the Queen Elizabeth centre as it was now known. So he sprang up in his seat and had to dash down to the lobby for his waiting driver. Mike arrived at the centre reading through his notes on the speech he had written a few days earlier. He walked in past security and up to the now, temporary chamber. After fifteen minutes, he was called to speak where he stood up and began to talk shop and muster support for his Falklands initiative. Half way through his speech, he said 'and that is why we must unite today, forward not backwards, for Britain. Because together we can make a substantial difference and prevent any future conflict. Our aim is better relations with Argentina and we want you to be part of that.' Mike's speech writer a young woman by the name of Jane Middlemiss was responsible for the political language, Mike just wanted to say, get up off your backsides and do something. However, was convinced otherwise by Jane during an hour-long speech practice session. There was a rumble of noise from his fellow Lords once he sat down. Slightly better than he had hoped, the place was not that full, if anything only about a third of Lords bothered to turn up. Defence was not considered that important, despite everything that had happened in the past year or so. Politicians still had not learned their lesson. As Mike sat there in the chamber, he could not help but think about all the MPs and their staff who perished in the Westminster attacks only a year earlier. He remembered the noise of the gunfire and the smell of acrid smoke for just a moment. It was not something he particularly liked and he managed to think about something else. Leaving the QE Centre he looked up to his left and saw the site were Parliament once stood. Now covered with cranes, heavy Lorries queued up to enter dropping off materials, it was truly a massive building site. Nevertheless, Mike had things to do, he knew it was By-election time; many of the MPs who died had not yet been replaced. Primarily because the PM wanted to show respect to them and their families, let alone the fact that, the public would not take kindly to political campaigning in the aftermath of such an atrocity. Mike volunteered to go down to South Croydon of all places in Greater London to campaign there for the new candidate. It was a safe seat, but Mike nevertheless wanted to be seen to be helping out. But actually, he gave a damn about his fellow MPs. Since the attacks Mike was so motivated to do more, he volunteered time and again to campaign politically and used every ounce of his spare time out on the campaign trail. Knocking on doors, speaking at town halls, delivering leaflets. It was a busy scheduled for someone in his sixties and Mike's right knee was beginning to play up again. Mike received praise from the PM at the party conference for being the MP who helped out most during the campaign season. To Mike he was embarrassed, he did not want any accolade. He wanted to honour the memory of those people who were brutally gunned down. 'To think' said Mike as he turned to his staff, 'over two hundred MPs killed! Two hundred! That is just unacceptable, and when you look at it, attendance for debates and public discussion is down year on year. What do we have to do to get modern politicians to take more responsibility and step up to the plate?'

For his tireless work for the country and relentless efforts, Mike was recognised in the New Year's honours by the Queen. He was made Knight of the Garter, the highest recognition anyone could receive. It would mean that he would sit at a round table of sorts, whereby only the most senior of Queen's representatives sat and met. Meetings took place more frequently now because of the serious threats facing the nation. The Queen despite her age, wanted to keep abreast of the thoughts and actions of her most trusted advisors. Mike was now one of them, he like Sir John Minors, sat at the highest table in the land. Due to the nature of what was being discussed, Mike had a security detachment sweep the room for bugs on a regular basis and install signal jammers around the building. Mike wanted total and utter privacy. Unlike the cabinet where leaks were an everyday occurrence, the Knights of the Garter, when they met, no one knew what was talked about, except those who attended. Meetings actually took place at Windsor castle of all places. The Queen wanted it close to her and found that this location worked well for everyone. The only problem was the public nature of the castle. Mike was concerned that Chinese or Russian agents might try to plant devices in the castle or park listening vehicles nearby to eavesdrop. But this never materialised. Mike however was cautious. He had the US Ambassador on the phone to him asking about the award and his meetings around a week after receiving it. Mike's ears would prick up when he heard the Ambassador come out with that. He was concerned that the Americans were listening from their satellites, so he had the roof of the building lead lined and various other radio signals jammed in close proximity. The Americans were well known for their mass surveillance and the amount of dirt they had on foreign dignitaries was incredible. It was suspected that on more than one occasion security leaks actually originated from the Americans via the CIA. Designed to destabilise even allies. During the meetings, Mike had flights that were taking off and landing at Heathrow, deliberately fly over the castle so as to block and distract any satellite coverage. Whilst on the phone to the US Ambassador, Mike asked for a meeting to discuss a range of topics, namely military co-operation. But the reality was this was political, he knew that he had to get the US approval for a whole range of things and wanted to keep them on side.

The Ambassador was an intellectual at heart, and not to mention multi-billionaire, he had taken up the role at the request of the President. They were both good buddies, so Mike knew that it would be important to keep in with him. Ambassador Tom Barry was his name. He wore glasses, was about five foot eleven, slender build, balding hair. 'So Mike tell me more about your new title, we are all fascinated about it here' said Tom looking out over Vauxhall from his new offices at the relatively new US Embassy in London. 'Well, you see, it is an ancient order that goes back centuries. The Knights of the Garter were considered the King or Queen's closest council.' Said Mike. 'You have been busy' said Tom. 'It feels like you have lurched from one crisis to another, and at the same time been busier that most of your Cabinet put together. How do you cope?' Mike looked at him and felt a touch awkward, he suspected the Americans had been watching him closely and Mike felt uncomfortable with the line of questioning. It felt like he was being put on the spot for his actions this past year or two and the Americans knew everything. 'Well thanks, I like a challenge, in particular, I like a challenge when it is about improving the lives of our people.' Mike wanted to convey the idea that he was not only a patriot but deeply passionate about UK PLC. Every aspect of British life Mike wanted to affect, but knew, he was not Prime Minister. Defence Secretary as he was still had a strong influence at the heart of government and Mike had managed to get a range of topics pushed through. Tom looked at him straight in the eye and said, 'what can we do to help you? We saw your scuffle with the Argentines, we also note with interest how you handled the Russians. You did not consult us though and that was a little concerning. Let me guess; now you want our help with Argentina and China?' said Tom. 'Well, we had hoped to get your blessing for sending a carrier task force down for exercises in the waters around the Falklands for a week early next year. In addition, yes, any pressure you can put on the Chinese to stop arming the Argentines would be most appreciated. Because the last thing we want is another war.' Tom leant back in this seat, rubbing his hands together. 'So let me get this straight, you want us to effectively say to Argentina, do not mess with the British and oh whilst we are at it, tell China the same? That is going to be difficult. Let me tell you first hand. We have a policy that states we are neutral on Argentina and as for China despite our ongoing trade war with them, our two Presidents are actually very good friends. So you see, upsetting the apple cart might not be possible at this time.' He went on 'What I can do for you however, is ask our Secretary of Defense to send a number of ships down there from time to time, smaller, unimportant vessels that just happen to be *en route* to refuel say to or from Chile or South Africa.' Mike sat up, and said 'that would be most welcome.' Changing topic completely, Tom said 'tell me, when do I get to meet her Majesty next? I only get to see her once a year, I would love, my wife would love to meet her more regularly.' 'Let me see what I can do' said Mike and with that he stood and thanked the Ambassador for receiving him. 'My door is always open Mike, I hope you know that' said Tom. Mike left the building after a brief look around the art installation in the lobby and then jumped back into his land rover where he was escorted back via Chelsea Bridge to Knightsbridge for lunch with the Emir of Qatar. 'I feel like the Foreign Secretary' said Mike turning to his special advisor Frank Callahan. 'The Qataris are annoyed and at the same time scared of you Mike.' Said Frank. 'What do you mean?' replied Mike. 'They know your reputation around Westminster effectively means you get what you want when you want it, and that scares them.' 'Well, let's see what they have to say. They are probably pissed about us stopping the LNG imports. What do they honestly expect? They have been financing terror in the Middle East against Jordan. Why on earth we are still selling them fast jets is beyond me.' 'Perhaps it is the Prime Minister who wants this to happen' said Frank.

'Of course it's the bloody Prime Minister, he is in charge. So we do what he says.' Snapped Mike. Frank sat back in his chair and kept quiet, the one thing about Mike was that he did not like or appreciate what he described as loose talk from his staff. He much rather have yes or no answers. Mike considered himself well informed enough to make decisions and these special advisors merely got in his way.

Mike was dropped off at the main entrance to the Mandarin Oriental hotel. He was ushered through to a private meeting room, where the Emir of Qatar was standing, waiting for him to arrive. 'Good afternoon Mr Secretary' said the Emir. 'Good afternoon Your Royal Highness, it is a pleasure to finally meet you Sir.' 'I can assure you the feeling is mutual. Please, can I get you something to drink?' said the Emir. 'Why yes please, tea, white, no sugar.' Said Mike. 'Please come, sit.' Said the Emir. And with that they both sat down at the main table, their advisors were asked to wait outside. 'So what brings you to London?' said Mike. 'The weather! No, only kidding' said the Emir. 'We are here to discuss a range of strategic issues. From our defence acquisitions to energy.' 'Yes, well, I can help you on both' said Mike. 'We are selling you 24 Typhoons and 9 Hawk trainers I understand? I would like to increase that number to 36 Typhoons and 16 Hawk trainers.' Said Mike. This took the Emir back, he wasn't expecting Mike to jump straight in and press for more sales. 'Why should we buy more from you?' said the Emir '24 I am told is enough'. 'Enough for now, but what about your wider ambitions not to mention fatigue, maintenance and operational use of these aircraft. We estimate in the RAF that for every one aircraft live on operations, we need a pool of four. So that means you could have four squadrons of six aircraft available at any one time. Six jets is not a lot your highness. If anything it leaves you short.' Mike went on, 'what we are proposing is 36 aircraft so that gives you nine aircraft available at one time just like our frontline squadrons.' The Emir stood up, pulling his robes to fix them straight. 'Ok so why didn't your negotiators tell us this at the time?' he said. 'Probably because they weren't thinking properly, also, we have recently increased our front line squadron numbers. That may be why.' The argument Mike was presenting seemed logical to the Emir. 'And the trainers?' he asked. 'Why 16 gives you much more capacity to train your pilots well and at a good rate. We would also like to sell you the latest in weapons for these aircraft like missiles and ammunition, counter measures etc along with an upgraded software and spares package. All in all this would increase the cost of the deal from five billion pounds to seven billion pounds. We feel this is very good value.' Said Mike. The Emir replied, 'let me think about this a moment.' He turned and looked at a painting on the wall, doing some mental arithmetic, he started calculating the costs and working out whether it was indeed value or not. You see, the Emir was in fact a honours student in mathematics from Cambridge University. 'Ok' he said and extended his hand to shake with Mike 'we agree and we will increase our purchase.' Mike was surprised he agreed so quickly, it demonstrated to Mike two things one that the Emir was trustworthy but also that perhaps he was in a bit of a tight spot now the UK had stopped importing LNG. Liquefied Natural Gas was big business for the Qataris and they had exported billions of dollars worth of the stuff over the past decade. The terror attacks on the UK halted all of that for Britain at least. The Emir sat back down and said 'we want to discuss Energy. How can we get back the deal we once had with you?' Mike went on to say 'unfortunately, we have a short term deal with the USA to import shale gas, which is cheaper and our strategic plan for the next decade is to stop importing energy and become 100 per cent energy independent. This is something that is now in place and will not change, not under this government at least.' The Emir, screwed his lips together as if to denote his displeasure at the answer he received. 'There is nothing I can do' said Mike 'as I say, we have agreed to do this on strategic grounds. I am sure you can appreciate the need for energy independence?' 'The Emir looked at him straight on and said 'of course, however, as a friend and ally we are surprised at the change by the UK' Mike looked up and said 'since the attacks everything has changed. We have changed. Moreover, your highness, we have concerns about terrorism in the Middle East, in particular the funding of this against our friends in Jordan.' The Emir replied with a raised tone 'these are lies, lies I tell you, we have nothing to do with it.' Mike was not happy with the way the Emir spoke and said 'according to our intelligence and that of the Americans, Qatar has been directly funding terrorism and we cannot abide by that.' The Emir stood again, began pacing back and forth in the room. 'Ok so we made a mistake once, we funded a group in Jordan thinking that we could help bring about political change. Just as you have done to countless countries over the decades, you recall well Operation Boot when you installed the Shah of Iran? Well, we had plans for such an operation in Jordan. It backfired and now we suffer.' 'That is the problem when these things become public knowledge. We can no longer be seen to be reliant on energy from a former ally, who now promotes terror. The British public will not tolerate that and believe me they are a tolerant bunch….I tell you what, I will make a personal visit to Qatar early next year to inspect the new aircraft you have bought and I will see what we can do. But I cannot make any promises.' Mike stood and walked towards the Emir, 'I thank you for your time today, but I must be off. I will have my advisor write up the paper work and contact BAE Systems about the new deal.' The Emir looked, shook his hand and said 'very well my friend, I look forward to welcoming you myself. We will sign the deal and begin payments shortly.' Mike walked out of the room, spoke briefly with his aide and then headed out to the back entrance of the Mandarin to his awaiting car. Off he went back to Whitehall, en route, he called the PM 'Harry its me. Some news for you, I managed to increase the sale of aircraft to Qatar from five to seven billion which is good news. They were not happy about the LNG cancellation but I explained British public opinion etc.' Albrighton intervened 'good stuff Mike, tell me about it when you get back.' Albrighton hung up. Mike looked at his phone in surprise and put it away. Traffic was especially slow around the Mall, Park Lane was being dug up for cycle lanes, and this infuriated Mike. He could not stand cyclists, particularly those that impacted road traffic users. The problem was the PM was a massive fan of cycling. At practically every opportunity, the PM was issuing directives for councils to dig up roads and install cycle lanes, much to the frustration of local councils and for the matter auto manufacturers who were beginning to question, openly the support for the automotive industry as a whole. One headline read 'PM shuns car industry for bikes', another read 'Britain to become the new China, as the PM wants bikes for all'. The green lobby loved it. The problem was that to most British people, cycling was simply impractical. London had become grid locked with all the new cycle lanes and cycle usage had only gone up around ten per cent. Mike often found himself stuck in traffic trying to get around the city. Sometimes he opted to walk, particularly the short distances around Whitehall. Once Mike arrived back at the office, he picked up his paper work that he needed to read on expanding the F35 fast jet fleet and improved accommodation for the Army. He then walked across the road to see the PM and update him first hand on the meeting that had been held. PM Albrighton did not appear to be vaguely interested, Qatar was in his own words a 'piddly little country' and one that no longer had any strategic value. Mike had underlined the increased sale of aircraft and the benefits to jobs and industry in the UK. But still, the PM, was more interested in UK current affairs. Albrighton had a general election to fight in a year and was looking at formulating new policy slogans that would resonate with the electorate;

domestic affairs took centre stage for now. So it was up to Mike to salvage what he could from the relations abroad. 'How does Building a New Britain sound to you Mike?' Albrighton looked at him as he drew on some paper. 'Yup, sounds potentially good, have you got anything else?' said Mike. 'Sure, how about leading from the front?' 'I think you want something that conveys power and strength, but at the same time is catchy and rings a bell with people.' Said Mike. 'I tell you what, if you could come up with ten phrases Mike that would be fantastic. I will review them personally, and we will get them out on the campaign trail.' Albrighton was enthused by Mike's creativity, despite being an old codger. This was however, the last thing Mike wanted to be involved with. The UK had valuable relations abroad, and this was often the case come election time, the politicians often found themselves engrossed in political gaming and left the running of the country to the civil service. No wonder things were often such a mess thought Mike. Mike went back to his office, on the way he bumped into the Chancellor or should we say, new Chancellor. The old one was often described as a donkey, cold and generally unsympathetic to Defence. The new chancellor was a smart chap, extremely well spoken and educated at Eton. He was fond of Mike and sympathetic to Defence, he often called up Mike to tell him about finance payments that had been made for military equipment, something the previous chancellor never did. Mike made the most of their brief encounter, 'how are things?' 'good' replied Chancellor Smythe-Clarke. 'We just got a new deal from Qatar, so we are now exporting seven billion worth of aircraft to them' said Mike. 'Excellent news' replied Smythe-Clarke. 'Well I must dash' said Mike 'got a meeting at the MoD' with that they parted shook hands and said cheerio until the next time.

Mike began the next week with a spring in his step, which was soon overcome by news that the previous couple of defence secretaries had ordered equipment using PFI Private Finance Initiative. This meant that the Voyager aircraft for example were rarely all available as they were used for civilian transport part of the time. With Brexit also having just taken place, the previous Prime Minister Rebecca Matthews had done some deals whereby the UK would buy European equipment, often inferior equipment for the British Army. Some of this had started to be delivered so there was no cancelling it and worse still the contracts gobbled up vast sums of cash, which infuriated Mike. What really aggravated Mike was that often military equipment was procured not because it was any good, but rather because it filled a political cause. Well, this time round Mike made sure that all the equipment that was bought did what it said on the tin and much, much more. He followed up on the contracts he had personally placed when he first became Defence Secretary and double checked that all the optional extras were included, like for example air conditioning for the armour. Often the British Army went into operations in hot, desert like conditions where temperatures reached 50 degrees Celsius, with vehicles that did not have air conditioning, this was something Mike insisted that be included as standard on all vehicles. It did become apparent to Mike that he would need to be in post for at least a decade in order to fully ensure that the new equipment he ordered was delivered, but moreover, that all the underlying issues affecting the military were ironed out. Mike spoke with his colleague the Secretary of State for Education in a move to increase Combined Cadet Force (CCF) participation. Mike wanted to bolster the regular army and increase reserve numbers substantially. To do this he would require a massive push by schools to help promote the military. This was controversial as many teachers opposed such moves, calling for their trade unions to block the move because it was inequitable with education. Mike managed to get his way however, as the Education Secretary managed to pull some leavers and get new funds for a campaign to advertise the CCF throughout secondary schools. The take up rate was high, with most state schools reporting a massive interest and moreover private schools too saw an increase in participation. This was the first time in years that Britain had had such a large standing, professional army and reserves. Mike set about a new drive to increase the size of the Navy and Airforce as well, not forgetting the Marines. The Royal Marines were a vital part of Britain's SBS however; their numbers had been chopped by previous Chancellors looking for savings. Mike however, was having none of it. He wanted to the number of regular Marines to increase from 4,500 to 15,000 with the equivalent 15,000 in reserve. It would prove again controversial, but Mike insisted to the Prime Minister that this be the case and rest assured the PM agreed. The general situation now, one year after the attacks was that Britain was in a much stronger position militarily speaking, although still much work was to be done. What impressed Mike was the efforts to counter terror altogether appeared to be working. The intelligence being gathered from the Kalahari had led to a number of raids across the UK over the course of the year and these had in turn prevented a number of copycat atrocities. Mike always made sure the PM knew that fact. The base in the Kalahari was beginning to attract attention however. A Botswana Defence Force (BDF) General was not willing to take a bribe and felt like he was being taken for a ride. One day he decided to drive out into the desert and came across the sprawling encampment. It was like a military base in the middle of nowhere. There were aircraft there, vehicles, buildings and by now close to one hundred personnel there. The General immediately got on the phone to his superiors and complained about what had been going on. Fortunately, for Mike, he had only six months earlier met with the Botswana Defence Secretary at a conference in Cairo. Whilst there Mike had managed to corner and speak with the Defence Secretary who went by the name Seretse Modibady. Mike had managed to convince him that it was in his interest to allow the UK to operate out of the desert for training exercises and to keep it top secret. So when the General got on the phone to complain, it was nothing new. Modibady said 'There is no issue, stop wasting my time with this and get back to work.' The General was gobsmacked; he really could not believe what he saw in front of him and got back into his jeep and drove back to Maun. Not content with the answer he received, he set about the long journey from Maun to Gaborone to tell the President himself. He was not happy about not being told about this and refused to accept a bribe. So it made him angry at the thought of his fellow countrymen selling out. What Mike had not mentioned was that the UK had also offered to invest into Energy generation via a solar power plant just on the outskirts of Gaborone. Not only fully funding it, but also ensuring that the energy generated went to power the whole city. This was a colossal project and one that generated much media attention, due to its sheer scale. Britain's foreign aid budget had been enlarged by former PM Dave Norris, so Mike figured why not use that money and put it to some use. By the time the General arrived in Gaborone, his mobile phone rang. It was Modibady 'where are you?' 'I am in Gaborone, coming to see the President.' 'Ok thanks' and with that Modibady hung up. The General arrived at the President's office, sitting in the waiting area. Only to tell his secretary that it was urgent and that he must see the President. The General was ushered into the office, where the President sat. Beaconing him in and pointing to a seat. The General sat down. 'Tell me, what is so important General?' Said President Nelson. 'There appears to be a military base in the north of the Kalahari Desert operated by the British.' 'Yes, I am well aware of that thank you. But what is so important?' replied the President. 'They are up to no good, it is an illegal camp and I must insist that it be closed and all those operating it, be arrested and deported.' The President smiled and said 'you cannot be serious, we have record investment by the Brits here in Gaborone, paying for all our electricity needs and you want me to close down a small little base in the desert? No is my answer.' Said the President. He went on, 'now leave me alone so I can have my lunch in peace. Go!' The General stood, saluted and turned to leave the office.

Meanwhile back in London, Mike's satellite phone was ringing, it was the QRA boys up in Scotland on the blower. 'Hello Defence Secretary, it is Air Commodore Howard from Lossiemouth, I have been instructed to call you directly with urgent news. We have had a number of unknown aircraft enter our airspace. Intercept aircraft have been launched.' Before he could say anything further, Mike jumped in 'patch me through to your pilots, I want to speak to them first hand.' 'Roger that Sir, please bear with me there will be a slight delay.' A few moments later, Mike was acknowledged by one of the pilots a Group Captain by the name of Hart. 'Go ahead this is Hart' 'Hart, Mike Scott here, Defence Secretary. Give me a situation report. What do you see?' Hart then replied 'it looks like four Russian Bears to me.' 'You what?!' said Mike. Mike was furious, he thought he had an agreement with the Russians and this was in direct violation to that deal. 'Are they still in our airspace?' said Mike. 'Yes and still heading South' said Hart. 'Right, can you hear me Howard?' Air Commodore Howard was also on the line 'Go ahead Sir'. Mike issued some new instructions, 'I want you to launch an additional four Typhoons and plot them on a course to intercept. I want a Sentry up and running, along with Voyager re-fuelling team. Have the rest of the squadron put on alert and ready to go Keep a track of them and record video telemetry as evidence, I want to show this to the Russian Ambassador. Keep me updated' Mike hung up. Within an instant the American Ambassador was on the phone, the US Air force at Lakenheath had been alerted to the Russian presence and had put their F15 fighters on 'alert five', ready to launch at a moment's notice. 'Mike its Tom. We noticed the Russians are back at their fun and games, do you need us to launch?' Mike replied swiftly 'no, not necessary, we have it under control at this time. Although if the situation changes I will call you back.' 'OK fine' said Tom, 'let me know if we can be of assistance, we have a Destroyer off the coast of Scotland on exercise at the moment with your HMS *Dragon*, perhaps we could co-ordinate them to intercept?' 'A good idea. I will have them move into position. Call you back in half an hour' Said Mike. Mike turned to Pickering, have Dragon and the US ship join up and head north on an intercept course with the Russian bears. Tell them to turn on their targeting computers and track the Russians.' 'Roger that Sir' said Pickering. Mike put his things down by his desk, and then immediately walked out to the situation room. A large operations room, covered with TV monitors and computers, in there was standing General Granville and various other senior officers. 'We were just about to order the same thing Mike' 'No problem, all done' said Mike. 'I was told by the Russians that this kind of thing would not happen again, and they have deliberately broken that promise. Get me the Russian Ambassador on the phone.' Said Mike. 'Sorry Sir, but there is no answer, his secretary says he is in meetings all morning.' 'Well summon him here this afternoon; I want a full explanation as to why this is going on'. With that, Granville issued the order to have the Russian Ambassador visit the MoD on Whitehall again later that afternoon. Mike found himself lunching with Granville at the officer's mess. They discussed many topics, including the immediate pressing issue of this air incursion. It meant that the RAF was going to be slightly stretched again, if and it was an if, the Russians were to continue probing UK air space. 'We will have to plug the gap somehow' said Mike. Granville replied 'Even if we order more Typhoon or F35, it will take some time for them to be front line ready.' 'Well, place an order for another 50 F35A, make sure it is the A variant, we want to make sure that the RAF has the larger, conventional take-off and landing version.' 'Will do' said Granville and they parted company. Mike heading back to his office for the meeting with the Russian Ambassador. Duslov turned up on time, but had a strained look on his face. 'Hello Mike, first let me assure you that this training exercise is routine and nothing to be alarmed by.' 'Why of course it is!' said Mike. 'We had an agreement and you have broken it.' Duslov interjected 'to be fair, agreements can change, our position has changed and our President now wants a more active air force.' 'Well, we are not happy about this, and officially notify you of our displeasure of these incursions into UK air space.' The meeting carried on for fifteen minutes and although brief, Mike managed to convey the point that he was unhappy fairly clearly. The Ambassador left looking the worse for wear and sped off in his diplomatic car back to the Russian Embassy. Mike proceeded to march across Whitehall to meet with the PM. 'I have just met him, the Russian Ambassador' said Mike 'I told him we are not happy about his Bears in our air space and he has said he will convey our message to his President. Who, incidentally, changed his mind and ordered the aircraft there in the first place, despite our deal.' Harry Albrighton looked up and said, 'you did the right thing, perhaps it is time I met with the President and had a proper chat about things. I tell you what, I will have my people organise a meeting, we will call it a diplomatic initiative or something and we will raise this with the Russians. In the meantime you carry on the good work monitoring the air space and we can discuss at a later date, alright?' Mike left the PMs Office on Downing Street and headed back to the MoD building. Mike needed to get some air, so he headed across to Green Park, where he found a nice bench facing some trees there were lined up to Buckingham Palace and sat down for a good half an hour. Just taking in the rustling sound of the leaves, the fresh air and people walking by. His security team was all around him, although you would never know it. Constantly talking on their radios to each other, it was something that amused Mike. All this effort to protect him. Mike decided that he would take a walk around and head over to Buckingham Palace to visit the State rooms. It was something he had always wanted to see, so after buying a ticket on his mobile phone, he went in. Security in toe, they wandered around the highly decorated rooms with the assembled tourists. Mike wandered around for a good hour and a half. He had decided it was time to do something for himself; he wanted a complete distraction from his day-to-day job, which had been highly stressful since he had taken over. Not only that, Mike was a royalist. He loved meeting the Queen and the Prince of Wales, but realised he did not know much about them or their history. Upon leaving the tour, he looked at his phone and realised he had three missed calls from the US Ambassador Tom. His phone was on silent and he had totally forgotten about calling Tom back. Mike dialled the number, Tom picked up instantly 'Mike, been trying to reach you for ages, everything ok?' 'Yup' said Mike. 'Well, I hear the Russian Bears have turned around and are heading back home.' Said Tom. 'That's good news. We will have to meet up again to discuss how we deal with this, and what else can be done.' Said Mike. 'We have the Russians off Alaska all the time probing our air space, so this is nothing new.' Tom confirmed. He went on 'are you free next week, let's put a meeting in and go over this further' Mike accepted the offer and the call ended, Mike walked his way back to the office through St James's Park. As he walked, he was deep in thought about what had been going on. He found himself jump, when a van drove past and its exhaust backfired. For a brief moment, Mike had a flashback to Bosnia again, recalling a time when bombs were going off all around him and his men. Mike could still smell the cordite and explosive charges in the air. Mike suddenly came around when one of his security team asked him if he was all right. Mike was taken aback but replied 'yes, yes I am fine'. The sun shone down on him as he continued to walk and cross the road into Horse Guards Parade. Looking to his right, he could see the garden wall on the back of Downing Street. He carried on through and up to the main entrance of the MoD. Mike was greeted by the armed sentries standing guard in the main entrance to the building. Since the attacks a year earlier, the MoD decided to have armed guards from the Army guard the interior of the building. They always presented arms when Mike entered or exited the building as a mark of respect. Once back in his office, he decided to get some coffee, he was not the biggest coffee drinker, but found that it was gave him a bit of a lift when he needed it. Whilst in the kitchen, he bumped into a young female officer. Stunning in every way, Mike could not help but pass comment 'New here?' he said. 'Yes' said the young officer. Mike made sure he checked her out, subtly of course. Anyhow, it was a distraction for him. As he stirred his coffee into his cup, pouring the boiling water from the kettle, the distinct smell of the aroma pleased Mike. He smiled. 'Nothing like it' he said. He walked back to his office on the way, bumping into to General Granville again. 'Situation appears normal, fighters have returned to base.' 'Good' said Mike. He continued walking to his office where he sat down and turned on his computer. Mike always liked reading the days headlines, so one by one he visited the websites of the various news publishers and broadcasters. He felt it kept him alive when he could see for himself what was happening, but the news media was what really motivated Mike, particularly now he was in politics. He knew that the media was essentially a weapon and if used correctly could get him what he wanted. So Mike unlike his predecessors, increased the advertising budget for the MoD to fifty million pounds per year for paid media advertising alone. He allocated another ten million for creative agency management, where all the creative messages and adverts would be made. This meant that Mike would have the very best in his armoury available to him. Just like a blue chip company effectively. Mike took responsibility for all the media; he had his people report into him once a week with updates. He found the drama around media a little tiresome, but nevertheless the strategic power it gave him was vital for the MoD. Particularly when it came to bolstering the military's image with the British public. From recruitment campaigns, to increasing the brand awareness of the military by branch, Mike ensured that each was represented equally. The results of this attitude towards advertising was incredible. Within his first year in charge of the MoD, Mike had single handed shifted perception of the Armed Forces from being a tired and fuddy duddy type organisation. To one of real brand integrity. Publishers and broadcasters regularly competed for the MoD's advertising budget and now that tens of millions a year were being poured into them, they really did start to take Mike seriously. Broadcaster *Global News* on more than one occasion inviting Mike to speak at a conference at Davos of all places for the *Global News* coverage of the World Economic Forum. Even Mike was surprised, but apparently word had got back that *Global* really admired Mike's passion for the media and wanted to recognise him over other ministers as a result. He sat on a panel featuring the CEO of Goldman Sachs and hosted by the Global Head of News for *Global*. They discussed topics ranging from nuclear proliferation to the environment. Each time the *Global News* presenter asking what Mike thought and why, particularly from a military perspective. Mike tried to keep it light and not go to heavy on the war side of things, rather, opting for political answers and he found that seemed to work well with the audience. An audience made up of mainly financiers. Once the debate was over, Mike found himself being bombarded with questions from the audience and countless attendees trying to give him their business cards. Mike allowed security to let them through. And he slowly one by one collected around thirty business cards in total. Eleven of which had offers for him to become a non-executive director of their firm. Being associated with Goldman Sachs was big business and reputation meant everything. From fund managers, to asset managers to private equity to family offices. Mike found himself at the centre of a very lucrative world. Even the CEO of Goldman's asked Mike if he would like to join the board in the UK. To which Mike kindly accepted his offer. In each instance Mike made it clear that he would not give them preferential treatment. This did not seem to phase any of the financiers one bit. It was particularly cold in Davos, with six feet of snow everywhere. Getting around the village was a nightmare, particularly because there were so many protection teams, let alone the fact that the roads were impassable. Walking became the best option. It was impressive to see firsthand and Mike complemented the organisers for their efficiency given the weather. But Mike was about to become even more important when the Americans arrived. Approximately ten helicopters swooped into the valley and landed. It was the President of the United States and his entourage. Mike found himself at a cocktail reception for leading politicians from across the world. In attendance was the President of the USA and the President of China. Mike was asked if he wanted to sit in the front row of the debate between both Presidents and whether he would like to ask any questions. To which he replied no to asking questions. Later on once both men had finished speaking, the crowd was able to mingle and chat. Mike found himself at the bar, ordering a drink. When who turned up next to him, but the President of the USA. 'Donnie' as he was known to his friends, was a fan of doing things himself. Particularly when most of the time, he had aides get this or fetch that. Now was one of the opportunities in a secure environment that Donnie could stroll around chatting to who he wanted over a drink or two. He turned to Mike and said 'Mike Scott right?' 'Yup' replied Mike. 'So what brings you here? I didn't know Defence mattered to these guys?' said Donnie. 'Well, I thought the same, but since I have been here, it has been fantastic.' Said Mike. The two men went on to talk for a good twenty minutes, both of them knocking back a couple of drinks as they spoke. It did not go unnoticed, with hoards of people circling around like a feeding fest by a school of sharks. Mike shook hands with the President and said, 'thanks again Mr President, I look forward to seeing you state side.' With that, The President walked off into the crowd. His secret service detail in toe. Mike had hit it off with the most powerful man in the world. Donnie took to Mike, his no nonsense approach. He also liked the fact that Mike had some years on him and wasn't some young gun trying to make a name for himself, he had invited Mike to Washington in a few months time to discuss defence procurement and the general partnership between both nations. Mike carried on hugging the bar and once he was rightly drunk, he knew it was time to head back to his hotel. As he made his way through the crowd, countless people tried to stop him and talk. But Mike apologised and said that he had to be elsewhere. Stumbling in the snow, he looked up and the heavens opened. Fresh snow was falling and it was bitterly cold. Mike and his security team made it back to the hotel. Where Mike proceeded to head for the bar for a nightcap with his security. They all insisted they could not drink, but Mike overrode them and ordered them to drink with him. One drink. Mike headed upstairs shortly after and crashed out until the morning. Mike was only there for a short visit and when he had to leave, he said to the pilot waiting for him in Geneva that he wanted to stop off in Gibraltar for some bacon and liver for breakfast. Mike was a massive fan of the Rock and had not been in an age. He ordered the pilot of this BAE 146 to change route and fly to Gibraltar airport. He had the pilot radio ahead and order the troops stationed there to be ready for inspection later that afternoon. He arrived in Gibraltar, sun was out, and weather was pleasant. He jumped aboard a waiting jeep and headed into to town for a great vantage point of the Rock itself. Ordering his favourite bacon and liver, he regularly ate whenever he could. The last time he had been in Gibraltar he had had breakfast with the late Sir Winston Churchill Junior, grandson of the great man himself. Mike had an inspection to conduct in the afternoon and wanted to speak at length to the base commander about troop numbers and equipment. One thing Mike was concerned about was that the Gibraltar Squadron for the Royal Navy had effectively been reduced to a couple of small patrol boats. Mike wanted capital ships like the latest Type 26 Frigate to be permanently stationed here, at least four of them. So he set about putting measures in place that once sufficient numbers of frigates were available, he ordered the four be permanently based in Gibraltar. He also ordered the RAF to have two permanent squadrons of Typhoon aircraft to be based there as well. To the lay individual this might seem strange. But the reality was that Gibraltar was a major strategic hub for the UK. Moreover, the next nearest base was RAF *Akrotiri* in Cyprus. Which already had a sizeable presence in the region. From Gibraltar, Mike flew to Cyprus to do the exact same inspection of forces stationed there. However, this time he did not step out for breakfast, rather, he focused on discussions with the base commander about increasing the number of regular Army battalions stationed there increase from two to six. This meant that there would need to be a sizeable refurbishment of existing living quarters to bring them up to standard. Mike in the end opted to knock down and rebuild the barracks there as this worked out as being the most sensible course of action. Mike concluded his talks and boarded his BAE 146 aircraft operated by the RAF. Mike liked the small and agile nature of this aircraft and told the head of the RAF that he wanted two more of these aircraft to be procured for the RAF. They were typically used for VIPs and the like, and given the strain on private jets Mike wanted more to be available for use at any one time.

Mike returned home only to be faced with a grilling in front of the Defence Select Committee. It was not so much a grilling, rather a bashing. What Mike could not understand was why so many MPs were angry with him and it turns out in the end, it was because he was successful. Successful in getting things done, in getting the military up to speed once more, preparing for war so as to sue for peace. Mike was a real expert at it. He began his opening remarks with a summary of what he had achieved in the best part of a year. 'Mr Chairman, I can assure you that, we have had great success in terms of building up the military once more. Not just in terms of manpower, but also in terms of new equipment and most importantly funding from the Treasury. As you know well, I have single handed managed to increase the Defence budget to five per cent of GDP, up from its questionable two per cent only a year ago.' Mike was interrupted by a Labour MP by the name of John Grimes 'what makes you so certain you know what you are doing?' 'Experience and plenty of it' said Mike. Lord Irving of Spithead was sitting in the audience along with Lord Maguire. Both men were impressed, very impressed with what Mike had managed to achieve. Even the Chairman of the committee acknowledged for the record 'you have managed to achieve much in your first year, more than anyone could have imagined. We wish you all the success in the future'. Mike thanked the committee for their time and stood up to leave. He turned and walked over to Irving and Maguire. All three men left the committee room and it was noted by the committee members that Mike had cross party support from the most senior and experienced politicians going at the time. 'Fucking wankers' said Mike. 'They don't understand a thing. If they had their way, we would be focusing solely on Cyber, cutting our infantry, ships and planes. And they would all be complaining about it. Instead, I have reversed everything that the Treasury had planned and more. This is the thanks I get. Oh well. Let's go get a drink.' Together with Irving and Maguire, Mike walked out to the new Commons Bar, which was a temporary setup in the QE Centre. They all enjoyed a pint together and stood around laughing at various jokes and comments about different MPs. There was very much a schoolyard mentality around Westminster. You were either in the in crowd or not. Mike was most certainly in the in crowd and his mobile phone rang. It was his secretary. 'Hello Sir, I have Goldman Sachs on the phone asking if you could join them on a discussion panel in London next month.' Mike paused a moment, 'what is the topic?' 'Debt and the banking crises of 2008'. Mike replied, 'I haven't got a clue about that. But why not. What is the fee?' His secretary looked at her notes and said '£25,000' Mike replied 'Ok put me down' and promptly hung up. The general election was fast approaching and Harry Albrighton wanted to get all his MPs out on the ground campaigning, this was something that couldn't be taken lightly. Mike had presented some ideas back to Harry as per his request and found that his 'Moving Britain Forward' slogan resonated best with his target audience. Knocking on doors was something Mike loved, speaking to ordinary people. Mike found himself out campaigning in the beautiful town of Wells, in the South West England. Knocking on doors, the reception was positive. Despite being in the middle of nowhere, Mike always had his security detail following him. Knocking on one particular door, the reception was outright hostile. He had come across a Labour voter who was furious with the Tory party and government for cutting welfare benefits. 'You Tory toffs, do not get it do you, we poor people have nothing and you are taking everything from us.' 'We all have to live within our means I am afraid' said Mike. 'Come; let us see if we can find a solution for you. Do you work at all?' The man replied 'no I do not work, have not in years.' 'Well perhaps if we found you a job things might change, you might change your vote?' said Mike. Mike extended his hand to shake the man's and the man initially refused. However, after some sweet-talking by Mike, the man shook his hand. Mike managed to get the man, called Kit a job in a local call centre, earning reasonable money considering. Mike promised to return in two weeks to see how he was getting on. When Mike came back, Kit was a changed man. Friendly, happy to see Mike and very grateful to him for getting work finally. 'I can't believe it' said Kit. 'A tory actually helped me. I am going to vote for you that is for sure.' These kinds of moments made Mike love politics. It was why he wanted to get into politics in the first place. It was what made him love Britain and everything about its democracy. Mike said to Kit in parting 'let's keep this between us. I don't want people complaining about favouritism or anything like that.' Kit hugged Mike and thanked him again. 'I won't forget you' he said. In addition, with that the two men parted. Mike did not have time to drive all the way back to London, so he had his team fly a helicopter in to pick him up. The Little Bird he had commandeered landed in a cow field nearby. Mike walked out across the muddy land and climbed aboard for a short ride back to town. En route Mike asked the pilot to fly over the city of Bath. Mike always marvelled at the architecture of different cities and loved the dramatic landscape surrounding the area. Flying parallel with the M4 motorway, Mike flew past the old RAF *Lyneham* air base, which was now being transformed, into a brand new regional airport for low cost airlines. The previous chancellor had wanted to build houses on the land, but Mike managed to convince the new PM the merits of having another regional hub located so closely to the M4. It also meant that he could land RAF planes there in an emergency. One of the problems that Britain faced was a surge in population due to vast uncontrolled immigration, the demands on housing were immense, although truth be told the Treasury liked the high prices as it meant they earned more through stamp duty. Mike was not going to get involved in that. Rather, he had his own housing crises at the MoD. With the increased size of all military branches, the need for new barracks was immense. The problem was the time it took to build these was long. Mike needed to speed up the process and spoke to the Admiral in charge of the MoD estate, ordering him to cut the build time in half no matter what the cost. Mike had the budget available so to him this wasn't a problem. Construction crews were working in three shifts 24/7. Mike wanted things to move much, much quicker. He had floodlights installed on building sites and brought in catering to give the workers a boost in morale. He wanted the new accommodation blocks up and down the country and overseas to be completed fast. At every meeting, he had in the MoD, he was always asking for updates on progress. Mike knew that if he did not chase things, the plans would slip, costs would rise and ultimately there would be nowhere for the new recruits to live.

Mike was getting ready for his trip to Washington in the United States to meet with the President and his team. Upon landing, he was met by an enormous gaggle of security personnel. It was America, everything was big. In particular, security, the convoy that drove Mike to the White House was huge. Consisting of approximately twenty vehicles, not including ten motorcycles. As the sirens blared out and the cars wriggled in and out of traffic, Mike got the sense that he was in for an important series of meetings. Not just with the US counterpart, but to meet his new buddy Donnie, President of the United States again was something he had strangely been looking forward to. Strangely, because, he had not anticipated the friendship they would stoke up. Upon arriving at the White House, the Defence Secretary of the US greeted Mike as he stood out of the armoured jeep. 'Welcome Mike' and with that, they walked into the entrance of the White House. Mike marvelled at the decorations and art work lining the corridors, as he was led up to the Oval Office for the waiting President. A knock on the door and Mike was in. Donnie stood up from his desk and walked towards Mike. 'Good to see you again Mike' said Donnie, 'Can I fix you a drink?' he said. 'Brandy if you have any please'. Said Mike. 'A man after my own heart' said the President. 'Two brandies please Jeanette. John do you want one too?' John Baxter was the President's defence secretary. A tough, resilient former Marine Corp General. 'No I'm fine with coffee, black please.' He said. And the men sat down. Mike was taking in the oval office, all the finery and the bust of Churchill on the mantelpiece. Mike knew not to speak first, rather waiting for the President to talk. 'There's much to discuss Mike, we noted, that you are building up the UK military for the first time in nearly three decades. Must have been one hell of a task?' said the President; he went on 'my sympathies on behalf of the American people for all those Brits lost during last year's terror attack, truly shocking. I understand you lost some good friends?' 'Yup, we did. I did. It was the single worst terror attack in our nation's history. Equivalent to your 9/11.' Said Mike. 'Well let us know if we can be of any assistance, I have already spoken with Harry a number of times and we seem to be making good progress.' The conversation went on for an hour. The President had allocated an hour for Mike, in truth the meeting went on an hour and a half. The President liked Mike and together they seemed to hit it off rather well. 'John will see that you get the latest assault rifle, you said you want 400,000 of them right? We will have the manufacturers of the AR-15 confirm the order, with all the additional specs, right John?' said the President. John Baxter stood up as he was about to leave the meeting, 'that's right Donnie; we'll sort the details out for Mike.' It was a massive order for assault weapons and the Americans were more than happy to supply to one of their closest allies. Mike was only in Washington for forty eight hours, so he wanted to make sure that he visited the memorial at the Pentagon in honour of those killed on 9/11. This impressed John Baxter and the two men then headed to the Pentagon itself for further meetings on the F35A that Mike had ordered for the RAF, along with a replacement for the Tomahawk, Harpoon and very latest Close In Weapons Systems (CIWS) for the Royal Navy. Mike underlined the need to get this equipment quickly to his US counterparts. The one thing he always feared was the UK Treasury and he knew first-hand how budgets could be squeezed at a moment's notice. Therefore, he signed deals ensuring that they could not be cancelled under any circumstances and he agreed with the Americans to be put front of the queue for all the purchases. Naturally, this eagerness pleased the Americans who had been impressed by Mike and his general attitude. The President signed an Executive Order ensuring that the UK be given priority treatment for the above equipment. When Mike heard that, even he was surprised. But Mike wanted to experience life on board a submarine for his trip back to the UK, so he had arranged a boat to pick him up at New York. He flew in to La Guardia, from there had an escort to New York City Harbour, where under the cover of darkness a British Astute Class submarine was waiting for him. Mike knew the intended route back across the Atlantic would stop in Bermuda. This was not just a sightseeing tour, this was vitally important. Mike set sail from New York and bunked down in the Captain's cabin for the journey to Bermuda. It took a couple of days to get there at full speed. Once the submarine had arrived just off the coast of Bermuda, a speed boat came out to meet it. Mike clambered aboard and was ferried to the local town centre where he met the Governor of Bermuda for talks on re-establishing a submarine base on the island. He also had a meeting with the head of MI6, who had flown out on board a C130J Hercules. Mike had understood the very important nature of the call into Bermuda that was making it a safe haven for spies, former spies and anyone being put into exile by the United Kingdom. Mike wanted to ensure that anyone who had sacrificed themselves for Queen and Country was well looked after. So Mike established a new top secret operation, funded by black ops, to procure a number of houses on the island. These were then made secure, top notch security systems, and had safes built into the walls, full of cash, passports and weapons. Mike wanted to ensure that whoever would be using these houses was set for life. Granted, very few British agents were ever sent into exile or to a safe house in Bermuda. It was considered a one-way trip and actually, the only way to get there was by Submarine from the UK if you were sent into exile. Mike only stayed on the island for 24 hours to ensure things were setup and ready to go. It would take a couple of months for the Head of MI6 to establish the plans that Mike had put in place. C had a number of trusted operatives get the job done. Mike was ferried back out to the waiting HMS Ambush and got underway again for Plymouth Naval Base on the South Coast of Britain. Mike actually enjoyed the trip by submarine to England. It gave him first-hand experience of what the crew goes through, he also got to speak at length to a Vice Admiral in command of the boat about the challenges facing him and his crew. The Vice Admiral thanking Mike for increasing the number of boats in the fleet to fifteen. 'It makes a huge difference to us, more boats mean we can be in more places and it puts less strain on the crews' said the Vice Admiral. En route, the submarine made contact with a Russian Yasen class submarine, which had the crew on high alert. For the best part of an hour the British and Russian boats played a game of cat and mouse. On this occasion the Russians had the upper hand, it was a little like a scene out of *The Hunt for Red October* starring Sean Connery. Eventually, the Russians broke off contact and disappeared into the mid-Atlantic. Mike was surprised that the Russians were operating so far out into the Atlantic without support, but he had heard of unconfirmed reports suggesting they were there. Now he had first-hand proof that they were there, not that there was anything wrong with it. However, what it meant was that the British boats would probably come into contact again with the Russians, at least they now had some experience they could share with other boat commanders. The contact with a British boat would have surprised the Russians. They would have wondered why one of our boats was operating so far out into the Atlantic, just like the British wondered about the Russians. As HMS *Ambush* approach the English Channel, a

Russian Anti-Submarine Destroyer, just so happened to be passing through the straight. It was an Udaloy Class Destroyer, the *Severomorsk*. Apparently returning from operations in Syria. But Mike was sceptical, he knew the Russians were smart, in fact, he would call them on more than one occasion 'very smart'. Despite being an older ship, it still had very good anti-submarine capabilities. It was approximately ten nautical miles behind HMS *Ambush* and would have easily picked up the boat on sonar. This meant that the Russian knew where they were and could then relay their satellites over head to watch live who disembarked from the boat in Plymouth. Mike did not want the Russians to know he was on board, as this would completely blow the cover and operation in Bermuda. So he set about borrowing a uniform from one of the crew and once in Plymouth Sound, where HMS *Ambush* docked, he got off as a member of the crew with his sailors cap on. He stood on parade as the Captain dismissed the crew and headed to one of the main building where his security team was waiting for him. Mike radioed ahead when HMS *Ambush* had surfaced in the Channel and said he wanted a Royal Marines transport helicopter to fly down from RNAS *Culdrose* and pick him up for taxi service to London. Plymouth had plenty of Frigates about the place and a Merlin swooped in and landed on the rear of HMS *Somerset*. Mike thanked the Vice Admiral for his hospitality on board the HMS *Ambush* and promptly went about heading back to London. Mike didn't even tell the Prime Minister about his plans for operatives in Bermuda, he swore the head of MI6 to secrecy over this operation. Mike really did not want any other politicians to know about this resort as he called it. Fine, opening up Bermuda as a new submarine base was one thing, but the lives of operatives, who once in Bermuda were on their own, was another. Mike in the end had to tell Harry Albrighton about his plans for Bermuda, to which he received a short reply 'ok' was all he could muster. Mike had been on the go for the best part of a week and felt pretty tired. He called it a day early and headed down to his waiting car from the MoD building and back to his residence just off the Mall. As he lay in bed he began to read about the plans that had been put together by the Admiralty to re-build the submarine pen in Bermuda. Mike was happy and fell asleep with the papers strewn all over the floor by the time he woke up in the morning. Mike had heard the next day when he woke on *Global News* that the Russian fleet was passing through the English Channel en route to Syria. One aircraft carrier, two Kirov class battlecruisers which were enormous and extremely impressive. A host of smaller ships followed. Mike ordered the Royal Navy fleet on alert and to intercept these ships or shadow them as they traversed the straight. He also ordered the RAF to have continuous air surveillance of the ships whilst in UK waters. Four Typhoons followed close by, being aerially refuelled multiple times. The latest P8 Poseidon Maritime Patrol aircraft also shadowed at a relative close distance. Mike wanted the Russians to fully understand that the British were ready and able. Not that it would ever come to that. Rather, for domestic politics, it made Harry Albrighton look 'strong' as news coverage talked of the UK's 'tough response' to the Russian threat. Since leaving the EU, the UK now had full responsibility once more for its territorial waters and EEZ. Mike wanted guarantees from the Royal Navy and RAF that they could provide 24/7 surveillance of the entire zones around the UK. Be it by Offshore Patrol Vessels, Light Aircraft and/ or satellite. Mike did not want to rely alone on satellites as this was considered the cheap option that the previous chancellor had preferred. No, Mike was having none of it. So he again found himself having to order more equipment in the form of more patrol ships and Islander surveillance planes in conjunction with satellites. The whole situation demonstrated to Mike just how bad a situation Defence found itself in. Having to invest so much into new equipment and manpower totally took him aback.

Mike had never been much of a sailor. So when it came to the Royal Navy, he always opted for the best advice he could find. For that he turned to Lord Irving. Patrolling the EEZ would prove to be a headache for the immediate term. Whilst Mike had ordered brand new Surf Search Radars (SSRs) to be installed along the south coast of England to monitor the Channel in its entirety. He did not have sufficient ships or planes to patrol the vital shipping lane 24/7. That worried Mike. Because he thought of all the years where drugs, people and weapons were smuggled to the UK by fast speed boat or small light aircraft from the continent of Europe. He suspected that. He wanted to close that down. Since the terror attacks that claimed so many lives, Mike was convinced that the porous borders on the south coast were to blame. As he stood in Portsmouth Naval Base on the quayside, waiting to board an OPV, he recalled a time when he was a child listening to *Winston Churchill*. Not that he remembered all the words, 'I think it was the general gist of it.' He said to Lord Irving as they both walked over the gangway to board HMS *Tyne*. HMS *Tyne* was clapped out; the ship had been used extensively and had little by way of maintenance or upgrades during its service period, despite being relatively new. Mike wanted that rectified. He wanted it to receive new engines, and have a total overhaul whilst the new OPVs come online. As they set sail for Dover port, a journey that would take a couple of hours, as they were sailing slowly. Both Irving and Mike took to the bridge to speak to the Captain and First Officer. It was the same story from them as Mike had suspected. An almost depressed Captain, despite now receiving the full attention of the Secretary of State for Defence. The Captain was disillusioned. 'I have been in the Navy nearly thirty years now and I have never known it to be this small. Not only are we unable to provide round the clock cover, we simply don't have the ships, planes or manpower. It is a disaster from a security standpoint. We have intercepted countless RIBs or fast boats over the years often full of illegals, terrorists and even weapons have been seized. Yet, and I say yet, no one seems to care.' Said Captain Bartholomew. 'Well, we are here now, and I recognise the importance of the Navy, securing the EEZ, so we are going to invest until we get it right. More OPVs have been ordered, but like anything these take time to build.' Said Mike, before he could continue, the Captain jumped in and said 'and then you have to train the crew, test the ships, before you know it a couple of years have passed and still we are short.' Mike could sense the Captain's frustration with the situation. Mike re-assured him that all was being done that could be done and after speaking with the Captain, Mike turned to Irving and said 'how quickly can we get these new OPVs out to sea?' Irving looked at him and said, 'I think you are already doing well, ahead of schedule by six months, so reality is at least another eighteen months.' Mike said back to him 'that's just not good enough, we need them now. How about we lease some ships from the US Navy?' 'Irving replied, 'that could work, although you would need to train the crew and that takes time.' 'Well' said Mike. 'I want them available in record time, in the next month. I am going to speak to the Admiralty and the US Ambassador. We need these ships now.' They continued discussing a range of topics as the ship cruised along the coast, hugging the features of the land until they reached Dover port, where they docked alongside. Whilst on board the ship, Mike used his satellite phone from the Captain's cabin and called the Admiralty and the US Ambassador. He requested the Americans loan ten coastguard cutters to the Royal Navy. At first the reaction to his request was cold. The American Ambassador didn't think it would be possible. But Mike promised not only that the UK would pay, but pay well. The Ambassador told him to wait half an hour and he would call back. Upon calling back he confirmed that the US had the ability to loan the Royal Navy another eleven coastal ships, ideal for patrolling EEZ waters. Mike was delighted at the news. 'When can you sail them over?' said Mike. 'Why next week' Tom replied. 'Great, get them here as fast as you can'. Mike told the Admiralty he wanted them painted and crewed up for training the minute they arrived. 'I don't want any feet dragging on this one Jim. I want those ships painted in the RN colours rapidly and then out to sea within the first week of receiving them.' Jim Fitzpatrick was the First Sea Lord, and a trustworthy individual. He admired what Mike was doing for the Navy and gave the order for the RN to fulfil Mike's orders. Within a week of arriving, each ship had an entire crew assigned to it and re-painting began at speed. Once painted, the ships would in twos and threes put out to sea. Training began in earnest and each day, the crew learned something new about the ship. It was intensive training. But Mike had managed to chase things along every day and push to get these ships in service asap. Three months after delivery of the first five ships, three were already patrolling the Channel. Mike sent the Captain of HMS *Tyne* a signal and it read 'Captain Bartholomew, you have been promoted to the Head of Coastal Command, well done Admiral! As you no doubt now know, we have five loaned patrols ships under RN ensign, with a further six to follow in the coming months. We will be able to monitor our EEZ, far better than before. I trust you will keep me updated. Mike'. When Captain Bartholomew received the signal, he was delighted. Not only had he been promoted, he now had the tools at his disposal to make a proper difference. At any one time he now had four ships patrolling the entire south coast of England. Each day, his ships intercepted countless speedboats laden with drugs, weapons and illegal people. Word soon got out and it was not long before the national press started publishing news stories about the latest interventions by the Royal Navy. Whilst Mike had filled one gap, he equally wanted proper aerial surveillance to complement the RN effort. So he set about having twenty two new aircraft procured in the form of Islander's. These came online far quicker than the RN ships. As soon as the first aircraft was ready, Mike had it take off from RNAS Culdrose where they would be stationed and headed south west to Lands end where the aircraft then proceeded to head out to sea and from the farthest point south west of the UK EEZ began its patrol. The aircraft were fitted with top of the range video surveillance technology, which meant that they could always send live video feeds back to base at any time day or night. The conformal fuel tanks helped keep the aircraft in the air longer. The Britten-Norman BN-2 Islander as it was known was one of the best aircraft types going. It had naturally been modified for the Royal Navy, along with a host of sensors and excellent radar, it boasted a good range. Mike, ever the enthusiast, agreed to go up in one on a patrol. Mike was impressed with what he saw and delighted with the progress being made. The RAF was not happy though, they wanted the twenty two aircraft to be operated by themselves not the Royal Navy. Mike overruled them and said that as this was 'maritime patrol' the responsibility should fall under the Royal Navy. The same pressure was now coming onto the P8 Poseidon anti-submarine aircraft which had originally been allocated to the RAF. Mike would eventually shift responsibility for those aircraft to the Royal Navy as well, but that would take another year or so to arrange, as new crews would need to be established and trained. All of this organisation was tiring for Mike, who was now approaching his late sixties. He decided that he needed more outlets and things to do that would distract him from his daily work. Swimming was always something that he enjoyed, however, he needed to find a club in central London that could accommodate for him. He first stumbled across the RAC club, just round the corner from the Army & Navy club. Ideal for him, because he could go swimming first then, stop at the Army & Navy for a bite with chums after. The grand nature of the swimming pool at the RAC wowed Mike. He found the club's setting to be extremely convenient, but the architecture and design of the internal building really moved him. The swimming pool was adorned by these huge pillars, anyone who had ever been there knew of the grandness of the pool. It felt a little like a Roman bath, with an extensive steam room and sauna, he felt he could easily relax here. The only challenge was the crowd that attended the pool, members naturally, but it was sometimes rather busy for Mike. So he went one step further and had his people secure an hour slot for him alone. It did not phase him at all the disruption that it was causing other swimmers and long standing members. Quite the contrary, Mike wanted some peace and quiet. The pool was his new oasis, a sanctuary where he could go two or three nights per week and swim around thirty to fifty lengths depending on how energetic he felt. On more than one occasion he found himself sitting in the steam room after a good work out, breathing in and out the hot steamy air. It helped clear his head, literally. Something Mike had suffered with for many years, was the continual blockages in his sinuses. As disgusting as it seemed, it actually gave Mike bad headaches at times and the steam he found was the only remedy. Why he did not use steam more was beyond his Doctors who recommended he use the steam room regularly. Often, whilst in the changing rooms, he would look up and think of the times when he was a young paratrooper, the exercises he used to go on, the jumping out of airplanes. You name it, Mike's favourite was the live fire exercises and joint air operations with air support. The buzz Mike used to get parachuting out of a Hercules transport aircraft was second to none. He had his wings, and a few scars along the way. Like the time he landed awkwardly on his ankle and ended up twisting his knee badly. Mike was ever the enthusiast. Extending his right knee as he put on his socks, he could still feel the tenderness after all these years, or perhaps it was arthritis. Either way, it often made him walk a little funny. The swimming was helping no doubt, as it eased the pressure on his joints. He found that some weeks after beginning his training, the aches and pains throughout his body dissipated. Once all dressed up, he would leave the RAC club around nine pm most nights. Heading round the corner to the Army & Navy club he would meet with Lord Irving and Lord Maguire for dinner. The one thing Mike valued more than anything was his friends and their opinions. For too many Whitehall mandarins were careerists, happy to sell a bright picture, but often the opposite was true. Mike had learned this many times over the years in the Army. Having had the experience on more than one occasion to brief Prime Minister's on Defence operations. In particular each time he met the Prime Minister when he was in the Army, he stressed the importance of strength in numbers. He also stressed the importance of having investment in vehicles and equipment. Something that the politicians, including Prime Minister Minors at the time of Bosnia, just looked at Mike blankly. Mike had to push hard to get helicopters, armoured vehicles, weapons that worked. 'Believe it or not' said Mike. 'We don't have enough of anything and we need funds to be released to fund this'. At the time of Bosnia, Mike thought he got on well with John Minors the then Prime Minister. Although, in later years during Brexit, Mike's relationship with John Minors would become strained, particularly as Mike voted to leave the European Union. John Minors had become quite bitter and twisted over Brexit and found anyone who voted against the EU to be rather stupid. Or at least that was his opinion. It did not go down well with Mike. As Mike sat down to dinner with Lord Irving and Lord Maguire, he remarked how much had now changed since he was in charge. 'You know what' he said 'I believe, I have single handed changed the entire approach towards Defence.' Lord Maguire chipped in 'indeed you have, you have countless operations underway, and numerous equipment programmes and overall have totally changed the direction of Defence. Not just from a political perspective, but also the actual operational side of things, which let's face it, had suffered the most this past twenty years.' Lord Irving added 'to think, we have had numerous conflicts from Bosnia, Iraq, Afghanistan, Libya, Syria and literally every politician of every colour has sought to undermine and cut the military.' He went on, 'when you consider what you have achieved with funding alone, that is truly fantastic. What we have to do, is ensure that our successors have the same enthusiasm and passion to get things done and more importantly look after Defence.' They got stuck into dinner, Lord Irving opting for the Beef Wellington, slurping back a large glass of red wine. Lord Maguire on the other hand opted for the steak, whilst Mike went for the Pork. All three went through two bottles of wine in relatively quick succession. Once done, opting for the Port and Brandy. They laughed a lot, roaring, at times, to jokes about various Whitehall figures. It was an amusing sight to the waiting staff. They saw these three on a regular basis and became accustomed to their antics and habits. They almost knew off by heart, who would order what and when. It was like clockwork.

Of the many tasks Mike had to carry out, by en large, one of his most favourite was Remembrance Sunday. Mike would regularly attend, not as a Minister, but rather in the parade with his former regiment. He could be seen, marching past the Queen and Downing Street each time, despite, requests from the Prime Minister Harry Albrighton. Mike always led from the front of his Regimental gathering and each time found himself at the local pub off Whitehall afterwards, having a couple of pints with former colleagues from the Parachute Regiment. It was a bit of a logistical headache for his security detail as they often either had to march with him or wait for him at the end. Politics was a dirty game and Mike did not really like it. He liked his ego being massaged that was for sure, but there again, he was not alone there. Most politicians had a big opinion of themselves. Mike preferred keeping to his work and focussing on getting the military up to scratch operationally speaking. Attending political committees, speeches and rallies was a bit of a chore for him. Whilst he sometimes enjoyed doing them, he found the kinds of people that frequented these events to be highly questionable. On more than one occasion he found himself surrounded by yes men. People who were shameless in the political ambitions and who would say and do anything to get on. Politics was like that. Hence why Mike tried to keep as far away from it as possible.

Mike had spent a lot of money come the end of his second year in charge at the MoD and Harry Albrighton was beginning to get coldish feet about that. 'Mike' he said 'we need to talk about all this expenditure. Is it really necessary?' said Harry. 'Why of course it is, I would not have authorised it if it was not. To me we have had decades of underinvestment and now I am trying to make up for lost time.' Said Mike. 'But, can't we scale back things here and there?' Harry enquired. 'Nope, certainly not. The one thing we need to do is this, otherwise, you will have another terror attack on your hands, remember that? Remember all our friends who died? Well, I won't let that happen again. Not while I am in charge of national security.' 'Fair enough' said Harry 'you carry on then' and with that, Harry Albrighton had accepted Mike's position. He allowed Mike to continue spending money where he thought fit and that was that. As the Defence budget grew, so did the political interest in it. For many MPs, defence was like a dirty word they need not utter. But now, it had political support from the PM and Cabinet. Moreover, with a character like Mike at the helm, people wanted to be part of the team. Mike had countless, special advisors, MPs, and the like all offering him their CVs and what have you. It was getting all rather tiresome for Mike. He simply referred them all to his existing Chief of Staff and told him to reject them all. In fact, at any sign of interest in working for Mike, he had his team clearly signal that they were not interested. It put a lot of noses out of joint and actually began to get him some new enemies in Westminster. A handful of MPs began to stir rumours that Mike was on the take from big business and that he was not interested in Defence. The political fallout was beginning to gain momentum, particularly in the press. A whole host of editorial was featuring photos of Mike at leading financial services company's events. Quoting how much he was paid to attend as a speaker. Harry Albrighton asked Mike what on earth was going on? Mike just explained that there was a group of MPs out to get him, for the simple fact that he was successful. Albrighton had his people speak to this group to find out what their side of the story was. It soon became evident to Albrighton that Mike was right again. Albrighton ordered this group known as the 'rats' to back off and stop stirring. They did so, albeit reluctantly. What it demonstrated was the power of the media. Fortunately, for Mike he had that covered. With all the MoD spending on advertising, Mike was essentially buying off the media. Only the publications that Mike did not advertise in, decided to run with the stories. So to Mike it was small beer. But each time he walked past this group of individuals, Mike gave them a wide berth. Refusing to speak with them at any point. Even when they tried to make amends Mike just turned round and said 'piss off'. Westminster was like that, even despite the attacks only a couple of years earlier that claimed so many lives. The bitter and twisted nature of politics meant that Mike had to watch his back and anticipate where his political enemies might try to strike next.

Mike's personal security was a big deal. He was issued with a watch that worked as a security alert system. In that, if Mike pressed a button on his watch, it would send a signal to his security team that something was wrong. It was basic, yet effective. Mike tested the watch out on a regular basis. His security team requested that. So from his office, he would press one of the two buttons on his watch, and a red light would flash on the face of his watch. The security team sitting outside immediately detected an alert signal and came rushing in. It was part and parcel of the position he was in. The latest variant of the watch had a much more powerful battery and range. It had a GPS link in it, so he could be picked up by satellite. As for his communications systems, the satellite phone was the most secure device of all. Fully encrypted, Mike used this a lot. His standard mobile phone less so, mainly for private calls. The secure courier system that he had re-introduced to his department had not only cut leaks, it helped reduce loss of key information. Leaks were common in government; it was a matter of fact. What Mike wanted to do was manage that outflow better. On more than one occasion he made sure that misinformation was flowing out of his department in tandem with real, valid information. That aim of which was to try to identify who the leaks were and where they were coming from. On one particular misinformation campaign there could only have been a number of civil servants who were responsible for the communications chain. Mike ordered them be put under surveillance by MI5, who actually managed to narrow down the leak to two individuals. One man, one woman. Both civil servants in the MoD, middle level staff, with a reasonable level of security clearance. When they were arrested, they were photographed handing information dossiers about the Successor class submarine force increasing from four to eight boats. Complete nonsense, but it worked. The pair were nabbed handing the dossiers to an undercover agent, posing as a journalist. The Head of the MoD civil service was pleased that the leaks had been caught, but moreover, the information was not being sold to foreign powers, but rather the UK media. The punishment was quite severe; a clear message needed to be sent that would deter any future leakers. So both were sentenced to five years imprisonment and were struck off the civil service for life. Their pensions withdrawn and pay docked. MI5 ran with a PR story explaining what had happened to the media, resulting in relatively good media coverage at the time. The misinformation kept flowing and an official directive was issued for it to keep flowing indefinitely. That way, would be leakers would never know if the information they had was real or fake. Another change that came about was the re-grading of classified information and who could receive it. As for the two offenders, they were both shocked to be arrested as they had got away with their leaks for so many years, they never thought they would be caught. The changes that were afoot in the MoD were quite radical in some respects. Namely, in terms of pensions. The MoD increased the retirement age of all civil servants to seventy. It caused protests and strikes. But saved the MoD billions of pounds. Even Harry Albrighton was impressed by the outcome of the initiative. Mike had to stand up in front of the assembled civil servants protesting on Whitehall and explain to them with a loud speaker that savings had to be made and that moreover, their pensions were no longer realistic in the 21st Century.

Mike needed the savings to finance his acquisition plans for two brand new Boeing Business Jets for the RAF. These would be VIP flights based on the BBJ 737 Max 9, with all the optional extras including counter measures in the form of flares and chaff. Mike had a number of foreign engagements scheduled over the course of the year, whilst he had used the Voyager and BAE 146, these were to all intents and purposes operational aircraft for the RAF. Not VIP. They had some VIP trimmings, but these were not primarily built for VIPs. So he placed the order for two brand new Boeing aircraft, it did cause some chaos in the media. With headlines like 'Ministers splashes the cash on new planes' to 'Mike bets on Boeing for VIP treatment'. Harry Albrighton was on the phone, but Mike calmly explained that these aircraft were needed by his department and would be available for use for the PM and other dignitaries. The BBJs had air-to-air refuelling capabilities, specific to the USAF standard. Not the RAF standard, so that was a bit of a conundrum. Mike opted for the air-to-air refuelling capability, even though British aircraft could not refuel it because the USAF had a huge network of refueller aircraft worldwide. Mike knew that in all likelihood he could call upon the USAF should the need arise. But this also proved controversial, with headlines popping up in the form of 'planes that can't refuel ordered by MoD'. This shopping spree by the MoD was part of a wider deal with Boeing and discounts were afforded to the UK as a result. It took a whole year before the first aircraft was available. It landed at RAF *Northolt* with a brand new RAF livery. Mike was the first to inspect the plane itself. He and his team were impressed by what they saw. Although as with anything new, it would take some time for air crews to be trained to operate the aircraft. This irked Mike as he had pushed for crews to be trained ahead of delivery, they still weren't ready. The VIP cabin and interior was first class. With a brand new bedroom and bathroom with shower. To meeting rooms with huge comfortable seats. To situation rooms with all the latest gadgets, giant TV screens and mod cons. The plane was so much more spacious as well. He knew this would go down well with Harry Albrighton and low behold he was right. Harry had to fly to the Middle East for a peace conference in Amman, Jordan a month later. He took the BBJ for its first flight and the first thing he did from his private bedroom was call Mike on his satellite phone. 'Mike! You're a genius, between you and me I am delighted. But keep that between us. We will get the Treasury to fund this for sure.' It was a huge sigh of relief for Mike, despite being relatively unphased by most things. This had attracted a lot of political criticism and the pressure had been on him to deliver. Harry's flight to Jordan was smooth and very comfortable. It made a huge difference to the image of UK PLC to have a Jet specifically designated for VIP flight. Even the King of Jordan, remarked on the plane, once he saw it land at Amman International Airport. The King congratulated Harry Albrighton for having the foresight to order such a plane, not because it was flashy, but rather, because it said everything about the intent of the UK. The country was declining in world GDP standings. From the turn of the 20th Century to the beginning of the 21st Century, the UK had gone from number one to number six in the GDP rankings. Harry Albrighton was on a mission to rebuild, renew and relaunch the UK on the world stage. He wanted to boost the economy and grow it once more. He knew that in order to become far more dynamic, he would need to export more, spend less on welfare and encourage work. But most of all, he knew he had to dominate the media. Albrighton was a great PR man; he knew the industry in and out. He knew how to PR himself, his government and his achievements. He wanted the summit in Amman to go well and to get the credit for it. A little like he did for the London Olympics that took place in 2012.

The summit got underway amongst a backdrop of political tensions. Israel, Palestine and the usual suspects were arguing amongst themselves. For years Palestine had been stuck in a political quagmire, unable to move forward for one reason or another. So Prime Minister Albrighton came up with a radical idea, it would be controversial, but what idea wasn't these days. Albrighton had spoken to Saudi Arabia and specifically asked that a large area of land near the coast line along the Red Sea be used to literally move Palestine to Saudi Arabia. It was hugely controversial. As it meant giving up existing Palestinian land to Israel and moving South to Saudi Arabia to build a new country. Not only would it cost a lot, it would take time. However, international donors were all lined up to fund *'New Palestine'* as it would be known. Enabling the people of Palestine to finally move far away from the conflict zone and start new lives. Initially the surveys found that sixty per cent of Palestinians approved of the idea. To many local people in Gaza or throughout Palestine, life had become unbearable. No electricity, no jobs, no sewage, it was terrible. Harry Albrighton recognised this and wanted to provide a lasting solution, which was simple in its essence. Yet effective for the long term. Moreover, would totally ease tensions with Israel and the Arab world and bring about a new dynamic in the region.

Despite all of Harry's best efforts, a former British Prime Minister by the name of Anthony Cook, responsible for the Iraq war, opposed the idea. He was being funded, or at least his foundation was being funded by the Saudi government and unfortunately he had the ear of the young Saudi King. This made life difficult for Harry Albrighton, but he still pressed ahead with the idea. As there was some support for it in Saudi, albeit lukewarm. The Saudis believed that the Palestinians would never go for it and that there would be too much opposition. However, they were willing to support the plan providing it was funded by the International Community and had the majority support of the Palestinian people. Fortunately as well, Harry's friend Donnie in the White House liked the idea. 'To me' Donnie said 'it makes sense. If we can't get an impasse with Israel and Palestine then somebody's got to move.' The Chinese also supported the idea, so in world terms it had the two major super powers on board. Harry was indeed set for stardom if he pulled this one off. For the idea to work, Harry Albrighton would have to visit Palestine first hand, namely the Gaza Strip and the West Bank. He would also have to visit Saudi Arabia along the coastline of the Red Sea, north of Duba and to the west of Tabuk. The Saudis had agreed that *New Palestine* would be the same size in terms of land mass as the old Palestine. So that at least gave the Palestinians something to play with, along with access to the Gulf of Aqaba and Red Sea. This meant that the *New Palestine* would have a trading route by sea, which would help support the local economy and jobs. It also meant that it could potentially become a tourist zone. A little like Egypt across the water with Sharm El Sheikh. The Palestinians would be given safe passage through Israel via convoy through Jordan to Saudi

Arabia. The whole world would be watching and the Chinese offered to act as peacekeepers for the mass move. *New Palestine* would have brand new electricity, waste and water desalination plants, you name it, the new capital city would be called Yasser, after Yasser Arafat. The whole thing was worked out, including a new border with Saudi Arabia and Jordan. Thereby creating a buffer away from Israel. But to the hardliners in Palestine this went down like a lead weight. They considered the Israelis to be the enemy and the ones at fault. But the reality was it was too late. With the World literally united behind a British initiative, there would be nothing to stop this. It was unprecedented. To have the USA and China both agreeing on practically every point was incredible. Harry Albrighton was beaming. He called up Mike because he wanted to have the British Army Engineers offer their services to help build new roads, buildings and key infrastructure. Granted a host of British companies got the green light to build the new country. It would be done in phases. First the new capital city, with enough homes and public services to cater for the incoming peoples from Gaza. With masses of cheap labour from the Middle East and beyond, Yasser was built in no time. The Chinese had also volunteered to manage the entire project, which was agreed by the UN and the USA. This was a long-term project, so building entire brand new cities was a massive task. Chinese engineers and architects were drafted in to lead the way and they showed the world how it was done. Construction was rapid and the quality of homes, buildings, shops, schools, hospitals was first rate. Once Gaza was empty, the Chinese swept through the entire region, going through every building to check people had moved. Royal Navy Amphibious landing ships like HMS *Albion* and *Bulwark*, along with the three *Bay* class landing ships of the Royal Fleet Auxiliary (RFA) were sent to help move the people to *New Palestine* by sea. It was a huge naval operation from Gaza, called operation New Move. New Move involved all the navies of the G20 managed by the US Navy. Every nation was willing and able to offer support; in addition, huge cruise liners were used to move the people. It took a whole two years to move everyone; Gaza had a population of 1.8 million people. The results were fantastic. When asked in a series of surveys what the new residents of *New Palestine* thought of their new homes, an overwhelming eighty-eight per cent of Palestinians agreed that the move was the 'single best thing to happen in a generation.' There were a total of 5.3 million Palestinians. It would be a colossal effort to move that many people and it would take another two years before it was completed. People were given lottery tickets and moved to specific new towns that were built in *New Palestine*. That way the move could be done in a planned manner and the disruption caused through Jordan and Saudi Arabia kept to a minimum. The Chinese deployed close to 500,000 troops to guard the route and conduct house to house searches. As a corridor by road was identified through Jordan and Saudi Arabia, this was managed by China. China showed the world single handed that it meant business on the world stage. Whilst Harry Albrighton got the credit for the idea (which actually was first aired online by Jack Cakebread and picked up by one of Albrighton's staffers), the plans were put into reality by China and America. It must have been the first time ever that the UN agreed unanimously, passing resolution after resolution on the move. New telecoms networks were installed, both fixed line and mobile. This enabled *New Palestine* to communicate with the outside world. It was incredible for ordinary Palestinians, to go from struggling to do anything. To jobs, mobile phones, the internet, homes, it was like Christmas or Eid whichever you wanted to call it. But it was a model that could be deployed again worldwide if need be. Attacks on Israel came to a halt once all the Palestinians were moved. Israeli bulldozers moved in and flattened first Gaza then the West Bank. It was slowly rebuilt to house Israelis, but that would be a longer-term project funded by the International community over the next twenty years. Harry Albrighton on the other hand kept coming back to visit and check on progress. He would literally camp out in the desert for weeks on end, it did prove controversial because politicians back in the UK accused him of not being interested in domestic politics, rather seeking fame and fortune abroad. To his delight, Harry was awarded the Nobel Peace Prize and hailed the award as a moment for 'humanity'. The award helped propel Harry forward to win a landslide majority at the UK general election. Harry's party winning over 400 seats in the new Westminster Parliament. His success was directly attributed to building New Palestine. He held state visits for all members of the G20 in one go to celebrate the occasion as he felt that it was a global effort. The United States was first followed by China, then Saudi Arabia. Harry Albrighton wanted to recognise the key players and actually he wanted to get in with Saudi Arabia, particularly as Anthony Cook was now advising them on a regular basis. Albrighton had proposed to the Saudis that he be the new interface between Saudi and the West. An idea they warmed to and considered over a long period of time. The Saudis were watching to see how Harry performed on the world stage, whether he had the charm and charisma, let alone contacts to sway the Americans and Chinese when needed. Eventually, Harry won the Saudis over and they agreed to name his foundation as their principal advisors on UK and European affairs. It was a coup for Harry because he had managed to knock Anthony Cook off his perch as the number one advisor to Middle East rulers.

Meanwhile, Mike Scott was busy back in Britain, managing the newly reformed MoD and was having immense success not only securing Britain's borders. But rather, chasing down terrorists who threatened the existence of the UK. Harry Albrighton was in London when King Edward III opened the new Westminster Parliament building. It was a magnificent sight, a newly built Parliament with a modern look and feel. The new site was totally re-moulded and reinforced against the enclosing river Thames, some years earlier quotes running into the billions were announced to battle the subsidence of Parliament. Now the new building would have solid foundations. It had a vacant space with a water feature and beaming lights each night where the mass casualties were found. It was incredible, the architecture and features were second to none. The cost would eventually come in at some ten billion pounds. It even had a new helipad. Harry would later receive the Order of the Garter for his work overseeing the re-building of Parliament and his plan for New Palestine. It was the first time in a generation that a British politician had managed to fundamentally alter a serious issue plaguing the World. The violence dropped like a lead weight, probably because there was so much political pressure from the superpowers. But also, because there were so many troops on the ground under UN auspices. 500,000 Chinese troops were a truly impressive sight, they remained in the region some years after the end of the operation to move the Palestinians. This caused some consternation in Washington and Israel. The Israelis wanted a swift withdrawal of Chinese troops from Gaza and the West Bank. On the one hand so that reconstruction could begin, on the other, because Israel did not like the idea of having so many foreign troops on its border. To China it was a strategic region of interest. China had major oil demands and wanted to demonstrate to the Middle East its power and presence. So China was in no rush to pull out, if anything, the Chinese agreed to leave a Garrison stationed in Jordan along the border of Saudi or *New Palestine* as it was now known. So as to ensure that no incursions were made along the Jordanian border. The Chinese Navy also had a presence in the Gulf of Aqaba, because it wanted to become the buffer between the Israelis and Palestinians. China had invested a lot in this venture politically speaking and did not want some suicide bombers or terrorist cell from Palestine to jeopardise the peace process. It went to the UN for a vote but was rejected by the

United States. So China made agreements with Jordan directly to station troops there. Jordan was indeed becoming rather crowded with foreign troops from the USA, UK, France and now China being based there. Jordan however was still suffering after years of conflict in Syria. Millions of refugees had flooded into Jordan for safe haven, but now Jordan wanted to start the long process of repatriation. For this to happen Syria first had to become stable and the war come to a swift conclusion. This wasn't something Harry Albrighton had thought much about seeing that the UK involvement in Syria was minimal to say the least. China on the other hand was backing Russia, Iran and the Syrian government. China again proposed sending in peace keepers to Syria along the Jordanian border. The aim of which to assist in the process of returning refugees to their homeland. The model used in *New Palestine* proved to be extremely successful. Much of Syria required rebuilding, and the Chinese were the best placed to finance and put into play the building process. They found the best way was to totally flatten towns and villages that had been ravaged by war. It made the process of rebuilding far easier. Homes, roads, utilities were all rebuilt by the Chinese. But at a much slower rate than that seen in *New Palestine*. China had started the repatriation process at the City of Daraa in South West Syria. The Chinese Army fanned out along the main highways securing the routes to and from the city. It was magical to the Syrian refugees. They were returning to their home city and it was as if nothing had ever happened. After Daraa, the town of Dael, then Izraa to the east As Suwayda. The Chinese had managed to secure the entire southern border with Jordan and began wave upon wave of reconstruction projects. It was impressive to see. All the major roads to Damascus were made secure and rebuilt. Syria was beginning to turn into a modern 21st Century nation. Although it still had a long way to go. Once China focused on Damascus, they wanted to rebuild the airport and much of the city's infrastructure. Blazed upon massive billboards lining the main roads in the capital were pictures of the Chinese President with slogans translated into Arabic like 'The Chinese President salutes you', 'China stands with Syria', 'Long live China and Syria'. Propaganda was an important tool in this process. Unlike with *New Palestine* there was no public consultation, this was take it or leave it stuff. The media and main TV broadcasters ran 24/7 reports on the reconstruction efforts and how Syria was being transformed from a war torn nation, to one victorious and free.

Never one to miss out on all the fun, Mike Scott had aerial and satellite surveillance monitor the movement of people from Jordan back into Syria. These enormous sprawling tent cities along the Jordan/ Syria border were gradually being dismantled as people returned home. What struck Mike was the efficiency and speed of the Chinese advance. It was truly impressive he thought. Mike went out to visit British troops stationed in Jordan and watched a number of exercises take place. A little like a scene out of *Charlie Wilson's War*, Mike visited the refugee camps and was taken aback by the scale of the suffering and plight of the Syrian people. There was nothing however that he could do, except continue to monitor the situation from afar.

The US Navy on the other hand wanted to keep pressure on China in the region and send its Atlantic Fleet on a visit to Beirut in Lebanon. It was a good will visit, one where thousands of US sailors would volunteer for reconstruction efforts. Miniscule by comparison to the Chinese efforts in the region. But nevertheless five thousand US Navy personnel made a lot of impact on Beirut and got to work rebuilding schools, roads and helping to repair the power grid. One of the major problems that Beirut faced was the huge levels of waste and rubbish that was accumulating in the streets due to poor waste management by the government. So the Admiral of the US Navy Atlantic Fleet or Second Fleet as it was known, put in a request to the Foreign

Aid departments of the US, UK France and Germany to fund three waste to electricity power plants in Beirut. The idea was slow to get off the ground, despite being urgently needed. Waste to electricity plants were useful, in particular, they would help eradicate the mountains of rubbish that had grown along most roads in Beirut. It was a major sanitation problem and the Lebanese government did not have the funds to pay for these plants. The western powers finally agreed a year later to fund the project, but it would take another four years before these plants were up and running. Nothing short of a miracle really for the people of Beirut, a long and tiresome wait for a solution that could have been done much sooner.

The Middle East had become the new PR battle ground after years of war in Iraq and Syria, both the US and China were on competing initiatives to win over the hearts and minds of the local peoples in the region. Both the US and China made use of the respective militaries to these ends, but also the vast commercial sectors that would help on the financing, reconstruction and maintenance of these new towns and cities. Oil was becoming much more important to the Chinese economy and the need to satisfy that insatiable demand was growing by the year. America, now a net exporter of oil and gas did not have the same problem. Moreover, a directive by previous administrations to stop the reliance strategically on Middle East Oil meant that the US no longer needed to keep such a heavy presence in the region. Mike Scott now in his early seventies, was still Defence Secretary and running the show well back in Britain. He did however; manage to convince the UK Department for International Aid to fund new power stations in Lebanon, Jordan and Iraq. Basic sanitation was suffering as much of the sewage network no longer functioned due to the lack of investment over the years. So Mike wanted the UK to invest heavily in rebuilding where it could, key infrastructure. Mike knew that securing peace abroad, would indeed help in the fight against terror. Particularly helping to reduce the radicalisation of terrorists. Avoiding conflict was Mike's main aim and that is why he insisted on investing so heavily in defence in the first instance. Thanks to his success with getting funding for the new power stations, Mike was also put in charge of the International Aid budget. Invariably more often than not, when a crisis erupted somewhere around the globe, the first responders were usually the military. Therefore, it was felt that combining these two budgets would make a better impact when it came to short, medium and long-term responses. Unfortunately, for him, this did not come without controversy. Countless MPs stood up in the new House of Commons to complain of the quote 'militarisation of aid'. To Mike this just demonstrated their total ignorance in the matters of world affairs. When challenged to make a statement in the House of Lords, Mike took his usual charm offensive on the domestic stage and told the complainers to 'get lost'. It went down like a storm. MPs claimed he should be made to resign or even be fired. But Mike had the full support of the Cabinet and Prime Minister. He was not worried in the slightest. The main thing was the power station plans pressed ahead with more speed and urgency. Mike wanted to demonstrate to the UK that these initiatives were having a positive impact on the ground and actually making a huge difference to the lives of ordinary people in Jordan and Iraq.

Within months of the new power stations opening in Beirut, the rubbish problem slowly but surely began to ease off. Waste disposal operators had those three plants working round the clock burning the rubbish to generate electricity. It made a huge difference. The Admiral of the US Navy whose idea it was in the first instance was nominated and received the Nobel Peace Prize. It propelled him into politics and he took up a seat in the Senate. President Donald Masterson liked rewarding people that made a difference. He did not like your atypical politician, with no opinion or personality. He wanted people with opinions and personality, the complete opposite. It did prove controversial and on more than one occasion, he installed a number of Senators and Congressmen that caused a bit of upheaval in the press. Donald Masterson was coming to the end of his second term as President and was already on the lookout for a replacement for himself. He sounded out the Admiral, a man by the name of Michael Benedict, Admiral Mike Benedict or 'Dirk' as his nickname went in the fleet. Dirk was a strong, imposing man, not afraid to air an opinion and was one of the few military leaders who actually got political affairs. Dirk had got the attention of President Masterson and he would soon receive the nomination to not only become a Senator, but also to be the Presidential candidate for the Republican Party. The US economy was booming after President Masterson's economic policies had taken hold. GDP growth was averaging four per cent each year of his second term in office. Red tape and regulations had been slashed, making businesses far more competitive and able to reinvest their profits as they saw fit. Government interference was at an all time low. Admiral 'Dirk' Benedict was a former F18 Super Hornet pilot for the US Navy. Once his flying days were over, he had applied to become an aircraft carrier Captain. After eight years as Captain of the aircraft carrier Ronald Reagan, he was appointed Admiral. Admiral Benedict was also a very good PR man. He had charisma and charm, accompanied with an astute ability to be in the right place in the right time. President Donald Masterson appointed Benedict to be his Defence advisor to give him some high profile visibility with the US public in the run up to the Presidential elections. Talking on numerous chat shows and news hour presentations, Benedict took to politics, like a duck to water. He knew how not to commit himself to over commenting, but at the same time wanting to air views that connected him with his voter base. To Benedict, he wanted to appeal outside his traditional voter base. He knew that he had strong views on international affairs, the economy and defence. But wanted to develop the health care perspective for poorer people. He saw firsthand travelling the globe with the Navy the amount of times his ship would dock in a foreign port to provide emergency medical assistance to local peoples in the aftermath of a Tsunami or natural disaster who had nothing. Benedict realised that you had to have a strong economy to fund everything from defence to infrastructure to health. He pledged that he would maintain President Masterson's economic vision to sustain the growth levels that had been achieved in the previous term. COVID was long over and thank goodness for that.

With the UK being the US's number one ally militarily speaking, Benedict had been introduced via video call to Lord Mike Scott who was still the UK's defence secretary. Although much older than Benedict, Scott still had his wits about him. They got on pretty well once introduced, they chatted about the upcoming elections, the state of the military and China's increasing growth worldwide. One topic that they wanted to discuss was the recruitment drive the UK was undertaking to recruit more ethnic minorities into the military. 'So Mike tell me, what is the ultimate objective of this recruitment drive?' said Mike Benedict. 'Well you see one of the things we have a challenge with in the UK is that the majority of personnel in the Army tend to be white, working class men. The political brigade in Westminster urgently wants to change that. But I have been resisting as long as I could for the simple reason that people should be allowed to join, not because of their colour or background, but because they are good enough.' Mike Benedict interrupted 'so you're telling me that the UK has now adopted a positive discrimination policy for the military?' 'Yes' replied Mike. 'That is political correctness gone mad, surely you want the best people?' Mike added. 'Our biggest fear is that the military will be infiltrated by an Al Saleem cell. Not only will the British government be responsible for training, but also potentially the arming of our enemies from within.' Said Mike. Mike Benedict replied 'that is why we have a screening process, don't get me wrong, we have had Muslim applicants and military members, but they tend to be small numbers.' Mike rubbed his hair and leant back in his chair and said, 'you see, Britain has a large Muslim population and it has unfortunately become politically necessary to appeal to that particular demographic.' 'Well I hope you have some good vetting in place, otherwise you will be looking at a terror attack in a couple of year's time' said Mike Benedict. 'Let's hope not' said Mike and with that the conversation ended. Mike had to excuse himself as he had an interview with the Washington Post to conduct later that afternoon and needed time to prepare his lines. Mike had requested stats on the Army recruitment policy and numbers for the past two decades and it clearly showed that both accepted and rejected applicants to the Army where overwhelmingly white males from poorer backgrounds. During the austerity years, they had record numbers applying to join, but unfortunately due to budget cuts, and the greatly reduced size of the Army, many did not get in. Now, the situation had changed, Mike was well into his stride when it came to recruitment, particularly because he was looking to recruit so many more new recruits. Mike did not care much for political correctness and frankly thought the whole argument over ethnic minorities could easily be overcome by recruiting another ten thousand Gurkhas. That was exactly what Mike did. He went personally to Nepal and spoke with the government there and requested that they supply a much-increased number of recruits to join the British Army.

Back in Britain, recruitment drives and policy wonks wanted to create a Muslim battalion, a little like the Gurkha rifles. Mike was struggling to stop this obsession with ethnic targets, he found the whole thing a distraction. But some of the newly appointed special advisors to the MoD were pressing for a one hundred per cent British Muslim contingent. In principle, Mike had no issue with it. But he feared that it would only take one or two bad apples to cause major problems. Mike was proved right when Military Police discovered a whole load of Al Saleem propaganda stashed under the bed of a new recruit. When they discovered it, they opted to put the individual under surveillance, rather than call him out straight away. Installing hidden cameras in the barracks and listening devices on his clothes and mobile phone. The individual in question did not have a clue he was being watched. The Military Police recorded everything. What they discovered shocked them. As this new recruit, was openly trying to radicalise other new recruits at every opportunity. He would try to recruit them to carry out martyrdom operations, somewhat similar to that on Westminster a few years earlier. 'Look, listen, with all the training and weapons we have access to, we could easily attack Westminster again.' He was recorded as saying. 'I tell you what, on the first of next month, we will launch an attack, I will get the weapons from the armoury and we can leg it south to London in a stolen car.' Unfortunately for him, whilst he had convinced one other recruit, another found the whole thing worrying and approached his commanding officer to report the incident. The whole thing blew wide open and the pair were arrested under the Terrorism Act. The press and media got a hold of the story through a leak no doubt, and the story caused shock waves throughout the military and politicians in Westminster who were for the first time since the attacks openly questioning the purpose of such a recruitment drive. Moreover, that they were lucky that this incident had been stopped in its tracks early on. Mike ordered that all weapons were made double secure and that live ammunition be kept in a separate storage facility to the actual machine guns and rifles. Thus making it harder to steal.

Mike visited the commanding officer of the Muslim Battalion and thanked him in public for his oversight and leadership in the matter. Seeing that Mike did not want to alienate good soldiers, he made sure that the officer was awarded a medal to recognise his forward thinking. This kind of incident was a rarity and it meant that the Military Police would be checking more thoroughly new recruits in future. Mike wanted to draw a line under the matter, particularly because it was causing a lot of conflict within the armed forces. The US Ambassador was on the phone to Mike complaining about the situation and wanted to hear about concrete steps the UK was taking to prevent this kind of thing happening again. It was much fun and games as it was deadly serious. Mike just took this in his stride as he did most things. After the ear bending he received from the Americans, he decided to head to the Army & Navy club for a spot of dinner. Roast beef was on the menu tonight and Mike couldn't wait. He was still doing his laps at the RAC club down the road and had built up quite an appetite after such a long day. He bumped into Lord Irving who agreed to join him for a bite and together they enjoyed a fine dinner. Wine was flowing, so were the jokes and Mike could not help but feel that for the first time in his career, he was actually feeling a bit tired. Not just mentally, but physically. Here he was in his early seventies now, still in the House of Lords, and still Defence Secretary. No Prime Minister dare touch him after his heroics of yesteryear. Mike said to Irving that he had wondered whether he should chuck in the job and focus on enjoying his retirement instead. To which Irving told him: 'don't be so bloody stupid old boy. This kind of job doesn't come around every day and here you have the opportunity to shape things the way you want them and not let them deteriorate as they have so many times.' To think that Mike had been the longest serving cabinet member in an age, a decade in post. Mike did feel immense pride at that achievement, but also he felt that he had now set the scene for the next Defence secretary to take over. It would be something he would revisit in the not too distant future.

Mike contacted Mike Benedict and invited him to visit *Portsmouth* Naval Base on the South Coast to evaluate the UK's naval capabilities. Lord Irving was also invited to attend the review. One new aspect of Mike Scott's remit was to ensure the history and heritage of the Armed Forces. So Mike set about raising funds from private sources and government to buy the old ships once sold off to Chile and Romania respectively. Three type 23 frigates and two type 22 frigates were to be bought back for the Royal Navy Museum. All five ships would be completely refitted and painted with three ships to be based in Portsmouth and two in Plymouth. Mike also spoke to the Submarine service about old Trafalgar class submarines and arranged to have HMS Trafalgar and Talent completely overhauled and shipped to Plymouth naval base. Their nuclear reactors removed, but essentially, they were sea worthy. Perfect examples of museum pieces and extremely useful additions to the Plymouth naval base and would not only generate revenue for the museum, they would reinvigorate the heritage of the Royal Navy. BAE Systems PLC was contracted to undertake all the work, having had a long history of supporting the Royal Navy. When Mike Benedict heard about the idea, he wanted to roll out the same heritage project for the US Navy. 'Wow Mike' he said. 'You Brits have really got it together at long last' as they walked through Portsmouth dockyard. Now brimming with brand new Type 26 frigates and the two giant aircraft carriers. Mike Benedict said 'we would like to offer the Royal Navy the opportunity to buy ten brand new *Arleigh Burke* class destroyers from the Bath Iron works in the US at a cost of £20 billion, including weapons, systems and support. We think this is an excellent offer and will easily complement your existing fleet, which let's face it, is still way too small for a Global Britain.' Mike mulled over the idea, 'let me think about it' he said. Mike knew the US Destroyers were very good and far exceeded the capabilities of the British ships. They would be an invaluable addition to the Royal Navy. Mike went on and said 'we complement the US Navy where we can, granted we are smaller but we can still pack a punch.' As both men toured HMS *Victory*, Mike could not help but think that Mike Benedict would be the next President of the United States and not only did he now have the ear of him, they were actually becoming good friends.

'You know, things are going to change when I take over' said Mike Benedict. 'Up until now the US has been focusing efforts on the economy and defence, I intend to continue that theme, but with more vigour. It is vital for the world that the US remains number one in the GDP rankings, we have seen what a powerful China has done in carving up not only the oil reserves but also many parts of Africa, South America and the Middle East. They are effectively the opposition.'

'We have noticed' said Mike. 'Don't get me wrong, we have seen a substantial amount of inward investment from China over the past decade or more, they are even expanding their footprint throughout Europe. That is why I have been adamant on encouraging US investment into the UK. For some strange reason, many UK politicians appear to favour Chinese money over American?' Mike continued 'But rest assured so long that I am in charge of Defence and have the ear of the PM, I will be pushing American interests first. But we really need American investment in the UK Energy network, if we don't get it, I can see the government turning to China.'

Mike commented 'Let us jump on board a helicopter back to London, we can grab lunch and go over some further detail. I would personally like the US Navy to establish a naval base on the south coast of England. If you station four ships here, I will take that as a goodwill gesture and will probably agree to the purchase of ten of your brand new destroyers.' Mike Benedict replied, 'sure, let's get on board, we can discuss further over lunch.' Lord Irving was also invited to lunch and thought very highly of the proposals. Lord Irving also on board the helicopter said 'I haven't been on one of these in years!' Landing back at Wellington Barracks the men then jumped into a car and were shipped off to lunch at the Lansdowne Club, Berkley Square. A private dining room was reserved for the men. Mike chose the Lansdowne Club because it tended to be quieter and more private for such a meeting.

The next US election didn't quite go as many had predicted. Joe Sullivan, formerly President Jones's deputy was elected President at the ripe old age of eighty.

Jack on the other hand was jetting back from Austria having spent the week there and also some time in Bavaria, Germany. He sat patiently waiting at Vienna International at the boarding gate, when what can only be described as a 'stunner' walked up and sat next to him. Clearly Eastern European, Jack didn't mind one bit. Another passenger walked briskly past knocking the lovely eastern European girl's bag over. Jack leant forward and caught it before it fell. Thank you she said in near perfect English. Although with a hint of an accent. No problem said Jack. She sat back in her seat not moving, leaving Jack to position her small suitcase. 'You know they just announced before you got here that passengers are going to have to check in their luggage' said Jack. 'Well we should probably queue up then' she said in return, 'I'm Jack by the way', 'Tatiana' she said in reply. They both stood and walked to queue that was already some twenty people long. They chatted for fifteen minutes as they waited and then as they boarded the flight, Jack asked her if she wanted to meet up in London to which she replied 'yes', with a grin. They exchanged numbers. She was sitting a few rows behind Jack. The flight was full of British chavs, unbelievable thought Jack, 'I'm having to sit next to this lot'. Tatiana meanwhile had messaged Jack as she sat on the plane ready for take-off and they began to chat or rather flirt via text. The plane took off and was actually early landing into London. Upon arrival they both met up again once off the plane and continued to talk as they walked briskly to immigration. Tatiana flirting now quite obviously and agreeing to meet Jack for a date later that week, it was a Sunday. Jack went on his way and they both caught taxis to wherever they were going. Jack had moved back to Barnes, Tatiana was off to South Kensington. Later that night as she sat at home, she thought I want to get his pulse racing and she jumped up and walked to her bedroom. Stripping only to try on a skimpy red g string bikini, which she promptly took a couple of photos of in the mirror. She attached them to a WhatsApp message to Jack, saying, 'what do you think?' Jack ever reliant on his Apple iPhone, saw a message pop up, only to open it and he was delighted with what he saw. A tanned, blonde, smiling wearing next to nothing. Indeed his heart raced for a moment with excitement. Should he wait or just reply straight away? He had had enough of games with women so he replied with a thumbs up and smiley face. She replied almost instantly with a smiley face and x. The problem for Jack was that he was going out with a girl from Austria who lived in London. They had been together for ten years. Jack thought he would play along with this Russian lady and see where it went, meeting up Tatiana later that Wednesday night. Telling his girlfriend that he was going out to meet a friend. When he got to South Kensington tube station, he walked out to Onslow Gardens SW7. Messaged Tatiana that he was outside her flat and promptly came downstairs. Wearing a short black tightly fitting mini skirt stroke all in one number. She looked hot, all done up for the night out. She said, 'change of plan', there was a black cab waiting and she knocked on the front passenger window. The driver opened it and she leant forward to say, 'Nobu please'. 'We are going to dinner at Nobu' she said to Jack. Excellent he replied, 'haven't been in ages, I hear the black cod is good'. She smiled. 'Hello by the way', and he gave her a peck on the cheek, followed by opening the door for her to the taxi. She caught everyone's attention, in fact they both did. Jack was a good looking man and held himself well in company. They arrived at Nobu and walked straight in. Tatiana had reserved a table and they were escorted upstairs to their table. Champagne was the order of the day. Jack and Tatiana got on really well, as they ate, Tatiana slipped her shoe off and started rubbing Jack's leg. He smiled at her and she smiled back. Jack naturally played it cool and offered to pay after supping some cognac. He was a little tipsy and so was she, although she seemed remarkably coherent thought Jack. As the waiter came with the bill, she got out of her Prada handbag a small purse and took out her Amex Black credit card. Jack noticed it immediately. She swiped her card and paid. Smiling at Jack. As they stood he said 'how about a drink?' she said 'you know, I'd love one. 5 Hertford Street' she said? 'But of course' replied Jack. 5 Hertford Street was one of the most exclusive clubs you could go to in Mayfair let alone London. There they entered and where checked off the guest list. Tatiana had already reserved them a spot prior. They walked in and were escorted to a table. More champagne flowed, this time Dom Perignon 'I can't remember the year' said Jack. She looked hot thought Jack, but still he played it cool and remembered his girlfriend. She was talking a fair bit and engaging too. They actually seemed to get on rather well thought Jack. Meanwhile two Chinese women sat next to them taking photos of the surroundings etc. Jack was always suspicious when the Chinese were around and yes, they too made eye contact. Two Chinese men arrived, smartly dressed and joined the women. Jack definitely noticed that he was being observed. Tatiana began rubbing his leg again and Jack focused back on her. 'Come' said Jack, 'let's go downstairs to the club'. They both went down and walked to the bar where they waited to be served. Jack took his opportunity and pulled Tatiana towards him and kissed her, she kissed back. It was good thought Jack, Tatiana also was happy. The four Chinese arrived downstairs and also hovered by the bar, Tatiana looked at them and Jack could have swore she nodded in their direction. She turned to Jack and said, 'I have some girlfriends joining later'. 'Ok' said Jack, 'sounds good'. The club was just getting going. The crowd was fun and lively. That was the good thing about private clubs, there was rarely any trouble and the clientele were generally high rollers. Jack was dancing on the floor with Tatiana, tried to kiss her again and she turned away. Then suddenly two women screamed as they greeted her. A gaggle of girls thought Jack, they clearly knew one another. And yes these two were just as hot. Probably Russian. Tatiana said 'go get a drink over there, we have a table and I will hang out with the girls'. 'Ok' said Jack, and he walked and took a seat. The four Chinese were at the table next to them, not appearing to drink much but engaged chatting to one another. Jack smiled as he sat down to the Chinese men and women only for them to ignore him. Tatiana and her two girlfriends, Anna and Xenia danced away, Tatiana, walked briskly up to Jack and said 'we are going upstairs for a smoke, back in a bit'. 'Ok' said Jack. The night went on and Jack slowly got drunk. Come the end, Jack found himself outside with the three girls and jumping into a taxi, one said 'back to her place' where they would continue to party. Jack thought he should probably sober up just in case he had to 'perform'. Drinking water at the flat in Mayfair literally around the corner on North Audley Street. Jack walked into this flat and it was massive, must have been easily twenty million pounds. Everything looked expensive. Xenia lived here with Anna. Best friends apparently from St Petersburg, Russia. 'We will be back in a moment all three' said, Jack said, let me guess they're going to get naked in his drunk head. Indeed, they all came back smiling wearing nothing but their underwear. 'Take this' said Anna, it was a tablet. Jack was like, 'what's that', she said, 'it will keep you going all night'. So he did. And indeed he did last all night. Not sleeping a wink. What a night he thought, no one would believe what he had just been through, but to be honest, he didn't care. Tatiana was asleep and he decided to get up and go. It was six am and the sun was already up, it was late July after all and warm. As Jack walked outside towards the Connaught Hotel, he saw four men standing around, middle eastern in appearance or Asian at least. He thought nothing of it being still tipsy and slightly hung over and continued walking. It couldn't have been more than ten seconds later one ran past him turned and stopped in front of Jack. He was holding a gun. Jack froze. The other man was behind him also holding a gun in Jacks back. The other two had driven a van, a Ford Transit alongside one jumped out the passenger side and opened the side door. 'Inside' said the first man. Jack shat himself, not literally, but was really scared. He complied with their order. They all got inside and the Ford slowly drove away so as not to garner any attention. Inside the van, Jacks hands were bound together via plastic bindings, and a hood was placed over his head. 'We meet at last Bin Ahmed', said a voice in surprisingly good English. That was all the voice said. Then they started speaking in Arabic, calmly. Jack asked 'what do you want', the voice said, 'be quiet'. It felt like an eternity in the van. Perhaps two and a half hours went by. Then the van stopped. They were at Hayling Island, right next door to Portsmouth, in Hampshire on the south coast. Jack was made to stay in the van whilst three of the men got out. One remained inside to keep and eye on Jack. The three took a leak in the house they had stopped at, then came back to the van, and they got back in. They drove round to a shallow point and took Jack's hood off him. 'Time to go', said the voice. They all got out, and Jack saw a small pier at the end of which was a speed boat, Sunseeker. It looked powerful. 'Wonderful' thought Jack. Not only was he desperate for a leak, he thought what a fool he had been to fall for Tatiana. He clambered aboard the boat, semi man handled by two of the Arab men who were both quite 'built and solid' as Jack would later describe them. The boats engines fired up and revved a bit. The men spoke Arabic again, all along one had a gun pointing at Jack. They started out of harbour and luckily for them the tide was in. On board the voice picked up a satellite phone on the dashboard and called a number. Again, speaking Arabic. The boat was now out in the English Channel, it had been half an hour and the boat was heading south west from what Jack could tell. Then on the horizon Jack saw a container ship or what have you he thought. As they got closer it was evident that this ship was massive, it was an oil tanker. It had just emptied its cargo of oil to a UK refinery and now was heading back to Tripoli, Libya. As the speed boat was right next to the ship a hoist from the main deck came over and was lowered down. It was a basket big enough for four people. One man stayed on board the speed boat while Jack and the other three climbed aboard this old rickety metal cage. Once aboard, they were all hauled aboard. The speed boat returned to Hayling Island. Jack was now on board a massive oil tanker. Hands still tied and man with gun pointing at him behind him. 'This way' pointed the voice. Ten more men were on the deck with automatic weapons, AK 47s to be precise. Jack thought he was in real trouble now. I mean he thought that from the beginning, but now he had sobered up. He didn't speak a word. They took him upstairs to a cabin where he was locked inside.

Jack's cabin was surprisingly spacious and had two port holes. He couldn't believe he had a toilet too. And yes, he used it. What a relief that was. An hour went by before anyone banged on the door. When they did, a man walked in with a machine gun, AK47 pointing at Jack. Another followed closely behind with a plastic bag. He put it on the table and then turned and went out. It was a sandwich from Tesco and a bottle of apple juice. Jack laughed to himself and then duly ate and drank it all. He wondered what would happen to him, he had actually relaxed a little and lay on the bed. Tired, very tired indeed. It must have been around two o'clock and Jack could see out the window that there was still land in the distance, the ship was moving slowly. Then suddenly the door to his cabin sprang open and the same two men were back. One spoke calmly, 'come with me' he said. Jack stood and followed him. The man behind him stuck the machine gun in his back, Jack was scared. He followed the first man through to the stair well, they went upstairs, one flight, turned left and through to a big meeting room where three men were waiting. One smoking, the other standing by the door, the third looking out the window. The man at the window turned and said 'sit'. His accent was English yet also a touch Arabic. Jack sat down. 'Do you know why you are here?' Said the man to Jack. 'No' replied Jack. As he spoke the man slapped Jacks face saying 'I didn't tell you to speak'. Jack was clearly concerned and said, 'you have the wrong man'. He was slapped again. 'That is where you are wrong my friend, we have the right man and the brain behind our dear leaders brutal death'. 'In 2012 the Libyan leader was brutally murdered thanks to NATO and you who conducted the entire operation, your ideas were used by NATO leaders to hit Libya!' The man shouted. 'My country is now ruined. My family dead thanks to you and you my friend are going to pay for a long, long time'. Another man walked in with a rubber whip. Jack gulped and turned to the boss of this group, 'you're making a big mistake' said Jack. Jack was whipped on the side of his leg by the boss. It hurt. Jack stopped talking. His interrogators wanted to know about his relationship with Mike Scott. Why he was such a good friend and why Jack was a part of *UKDO*? Jack explained everything, calmly, rationally. It wasn't good enough. Jack was bent over the table and the boss took the whip and whipped Jack on the back side. It really hurt. Jack screamed out loud. 'You are SAS no? MI6 No? When you were arrested by the police, you claimed to be this? We have seen the video footage?' 'I was high' said Jack. 'I didn't know what I was saying'. 'We don't believe you. No matter, the Libyan leaders family will deal with you when we reach Tripoli, then you will suffer. Take him away'. Jack was dragged by two burly men back to his cabin, followed by another two carrying AK47s. Jack was thrown onto his bed. Jack said nothing. He lay there for a bit then stood up and stretched his body. 'Ouch' he said out loud. It was getting dark and you could hear the engines turning up a gear. He looked out the window and the ship was moving a lot quicker now. It was dusk. Land was no longer in sight. The ship was beginning to pitch a little, the waves were bigger now. The ship must now be out in the Atlantic hugging the French coastline thought Jack. Jack decided to lay down, he wasn't *007* and he most certainly wasn't going to try and escape at least not until he knew more about his surroundings. Jack had been asleep for a couple of hours then suddenly woke up around midnight, with a pain on his left side from the whippings. The door then suddenly flung open and a man walked in with a bottle of water, threw it at Jack and walked back out. Back home, his girlfriend who was still at home in Austria, had messaged Jack a lot and was getting worried as she hadn't heard from him. She contacted Jack's family and they too hadn't heard from him. He didn't even show up for work. Jack's girlfriend contacted the police to raise the alarm. But the police refused to do anything and said it was not their problem. It was a medical matter as Jack was known for having suffered from stress. Jack's family knew he wasn't the type not to contact them on a regular basis and his family and girlfriend insisted something was wrong. The police slowly began a very limited investigation to tick all the boxes. Meanwhile Jack had reached the straights of Gibraltar, it would be another half day or so and he would be in Libyan waters. Jack knew he didn't have much time if worst came to worst. But equally he recalled the tiny prison cell he saw once on the news that housed former Libyan opposition prisoners and feared the worst that he would end up in just the same situation. Jack went back to sleep and when he woke the sun was shining through his cabin window onto his bed. He got up and the door suddenly opened again, remarkably, what Jack didn't realise was that the cabin had four CCTV cameras and microphones installed. The guard gave him some food and water and walked out. Four hours later he heard the anchor drop as the ship came to a halt. In the distance he could see land. Sun blazing hot and incredibly bright. The door flung open once more. This time two heavies walked in and grabbed Jack whose hands were still tied by the way. Two more Arab men waited in the hall way. They shoved Jack out and up the stairs to the main deck back towards the cage that raised him from the speed boat in the channel. There were ten heavily armed men on deck all with weapons, looking at Jack. They put Jack back in the cage and lowered him with three other men to a waiting barge. On the barge Jack then waited a few moments, whilst another speed boat came alongside. He was ordered onto the boat and off they went into Tripoli harbour. A short journey of about twenty minutes. Upon arrival in the port, Jack disembarked and had the hood put back on him. He was put forcibly into the waiting jeep and the convoy sped off. Jack was scared and genuinely thought he must have been dreaming. But alas it wasn't a dream it was another nightmare. The jeep came to a sharp, abrupt stop some ten minutes or so after setting off. Jack was taken from the vehicle inside a building and went downstairs into a dungeon almost. It was dark and cool. Jack found himself inside his own prison cell and had nothing inside. No bed, no toilet, nothing. Here Jack waited for a day before he was interrogated once more. This time, it was the former Libyan Leader's eldest son who conducted the questioning. There was a table, on it, was three knives, a gun, a whip, a baseball bat and a hammer. Jack gulped and looked at the former leader's son and said 'I had nothing to do with your father's death, you have the wrong man'. 'Shut up and be quiet' said the former leader's son. 'You are my prisoner now and you will never see sunlight or leave Libya alive'. Jack sat in silence, wondering what would happen next. His clothes he wore from the couple of nights before now dirty and dusty. 'I will ask you some questions, if you answer truthfully I will not hurt you,' the former leader's son said. The questioning was brief. Jack confirmed his name, address, who he was and that he once knew Mike Scott. The video was played of Jack when the police arrested him, 'so you are not MI6?' Said the leader's son, 'no never have been, I have applied to join but they rejected me'. 'Ok, take him back to his cell'. Jack was dragged back and thrown in where he lay overnight until the morning, where the next set of questions would come out. Meanwhile back in the UK, his family grew more and more upset and scared that something terrible had happened. The Police now investigating said they would do all they could and promised to search his mobile phone signal to see where he was. They found him in Mayfair some days earlier the night he went out. But then the signal stopped the morning he was abducted. So they decided to check the CCTV in the area and they saw to their horror, Jack being bundled into a Ford Transit van. It now became serious. Special Branch and MI5 were made aware of the footage. They all also watched the older footage of Jack at his arrest, claiming to be in the SAS. They wondered what was going on here and decided to follow the van. Hours later the police had identified the van heading south to Portsmouth from London. The police some 48 hours later would find the Transit van abandoned in a parking garage on the north side of Hayling Island. It became a major crime investigation and was escalated to the UK Home Secretary when it was discovered that the suspected identities of the Arab suspects was Libyan. But the police found no trace of Jack or the Arab suspects they were after, it was as if they had just disappeared. The police informed Jack's family that he had been abducted by whom they didn't know and where Jack was they were still investigating. His family were horrified and the police as a precaution ordered uniformed officers to stand guard at his mum, brother, sister and girlfriend's homes respectively until the matter was resolved. No one knew why Jack had been targeted, MI5 contacted MI6 to ask if they knew anything and they came across the secret files they had on Jack. MI5 were furious. The Home Secretary called in Mike Scott and asked if he knew a person called Jack Cakebread. To which Mike said 'no'. 'I don't remember anyone by that name'. Bearing in mind it had been quite a few years since Mike had seen or had any communication from Jack. A photo of Jack was put in front of Mike who was now in his seventies. Mike said, 'ah him! Yes I know him. I knew him at *UKDO*. Haven't seen him in years'. 'Well' said the MI6 Senior agent, 'he has been abducted by Libyans and we believe is probably now in Libya. But we are not sure'. Later that day, the Chinese Ambassador to the UK, sent a message to the UK Prime Minister Albrighton that he knew the whereabouts of a certain Bin Ahmed should he wish to know. At first Albrighton couldn't work out what the Chinese Ambassador was talking about, and it was only by chance, at a cabinet meeting the next day that the Prime Minister mentioned this to his assembled cabinet, that the Home Secretary chirped up immediately saying that man Jack Cakebread has been abducted by Libyan terrorists. We fear he could be dead. It happened in Mayfair only last week. A rumbling ensued around the cabinet table and Albrighton turned to his cabinet secretary and said 'get me a meeting with the Head of MI6 and the Defence and Home Secretaries immediately'. The cabinet meeting was called to an abrupt end. The Home Secretary said 'Cakebread is a former friend of Mike Scott, Prime Minister'. Mike Scott had only recently stood down as Defence secretary, so the PM said 'get Scott over here on the double'. The PM then called the Chinese Ambassador and asked what was going on. The Chinese Ambassador confirmed that Jack was being held in Libya, precise location to be confirmed and that he had likely been tortured already and was highly unlikely to survive much longer if the UK didn't act. Mike Scott who was listening in on the call, once it was over said, 'we can get the SAS to rescue Jack. Lets get them on board HMS *Queen Elizabeth* and get her to set sail for Gibraltar immediately. Get the Apache's on board, along with CSAR (Combat Search and Rescue)'. A squad of SAS men were helicoptered to Portsmouth Naval base where they boarded with their equipment the mighty aircraft carrier. It set sail the very next hour and had two escorts in the form of HMS *Dragon* a destroyer and HMS *Somerset* a frigate. HMS *Ambush* a submarine was also tasked to steam at full speed to the Med. The submarine had Tomahawk cruise missiles which could be very useful if needed. Mike Scott decided after he had been briefed with the PM and assembled senior politicians and security staff, that Jack had been the victim of a terrible crime and had been setup to fall as a result of being put under surveillance previously. It was something Mike felt strongly about and he decided to fly out to HMS *Queen Elizabeth* himself, ordering a second SAS squad to join as back up. But not before a bit of an altercation took place between Mike and the Prime Minister. The PM didn't want a rescue as it would cost too much, rather opting for a negotiated settlement. Mike had none of it and insisted upon a rescue. After much toing and froing the Prime Minister finally accepted the need for a rescue, Mike wasn't happy about the amount of time wasted arguing. Meanwhile, a chinook swirled overhead and landed in the back of Buckingham Palace garden, Mike was waiting there for it. The PM gave him orders to get Cakebread back in one piece asap. Mike never felt so angry that someone he knew, had been treated so badly. The Chinook flew to Heathrow airport where an RAF Voyager transport aircraft flew Mike and his team and the SAS and other military personnel to Gibraltar where they would meet up with HMS *Queen Elizabeth* in two days time. Meanwhile, the Chinese Ambassador, privy to Jack's movements and location, promptly passed on this to the UK Prime Minister. It was acted upon immediately and satellite surveillance tasked to monitor the site in Libya 24/7. The good news was that the Libyans had no idea the Chinese knew where Jack was, let alone the fact that they would pass this information on to the British. It made life easier for the SAS rescue that would come three days later. When Mike saw the building and compound, he decided that he would need more men as back up just in case something went wrong. The SAS had the element of surprise moreover, security at the building was limited so as not to draw too much attention even in Libya where it was still like the wild west. HMS *Queen Elizabeth* had picked up the personnel and equipment at Gibraltar. The Royal Navy was ready as well and a small taskforce set sail for just north of Libya where it would hold position until the rescue had taken place.

Who would have thought a Royal Navy taskforce would be sent to rescue Jack?! It was quite an incredible operation in the works. Namely because Jack knew Mike. In essence Mike was compromised but didn't care. Jack was going to be left to rot in a dungeon if the SAS didn't get him out. As the task force approached Malta, they stopped for fuel and stores. More equipment was flown into Malta airport and transferred to HMS *Queen Elizabeth*. HMS *Ambush* who had only just arrived at Gibraltar took on the maximum number of Tomahawk Land Attack Missiles (TLAM) she could. Mike wasn't taking any chances. Not only did Mike want to rescue Jack he wanted to capture the former Libyan leader's son who had kidnapped him in the first place. So, there were two simultaneous operations being planned. It was one of the more risky recent operations for the SAS. They numbered fifty men, Mike knew he would need to either helicopter in the rescue team and/ or get them ashore by RIB (Rigid Inflatable Boat). He just hadn't decided what was best just yet. Meanwhile Jack tied by the hands was looking pretty dishevelled. He had no idea if anyone was looking for him. Satellites were now watching the entire building, not far from Tripoli on the outskirts of town, which actually made things easier for a helicopter assault. Mike's plan was that two troops of SAS would helicopter in via light weight Wildcat helicopters, escorted by Apache gunships. Mike made sure he had extra support helicopters stationed on the aircraft carrier along with ten F35b which would launch and provide air cover / superiority for the operation. The second SAS group was now studying the movements of the former Libyan leader's son and they had a precise idea of where he was staying. Mike ordered the SBS to join and they were flown to Malta on a C17 transport by the RAF. Some fifty more men. Large numbers, but Mike knew strength in numbers was vital should anything go wrong. Once they were helicoptered aboard the carrier, the taskforce sailed in circles just outside of Libyan search radars and territorial waters. Mike knew Libya had just installed a brand-new radar station just next to Tripoli. He wanted that disabled so the entire taskforce could make an illegal incursion into Libyan waters and get closer the night of the operation. So now he had three missions, first rescue Jack, second capture the son, third disable the radar station (without blowing it up). The radar station raid would consist of eight SBS men. Tasked to break in and reprogramme the radar to look down to the ground in the opposite direction, i.e. southward, yet still function without setting off any alarms. There was some Libyan army, security at the radar station. The SBS would infiltrate at night, midnight to be precise, by speed boat and make an incursion up the rocks to the station. There were six armed guards on duty at any one time and security was taking half seriously. The plan was to sneak in, two snipers would cover, the six other SBS men as they broke into the station. A distraction would take place at the main gate via paid local informants of the British Embassy. Arab speakers, hell they were Arab locals who went up to the station pretending to be lost on a night out. Four local men. It was kind of risky but Tripoli's night life was picking up once more. As the men approached the main gate, the SBS would cut the fence on the north side and sneak in pitch black. There were multiple entry points to the station. One facing North. This is where they would enter, it would be late so there wouldn't be anyone operating the station at that time. They would get to the control room and reprogramme the radar search functionality. It was a Lockheed Martin Surf Search Radar that had recently been installed by the Americans. Operating panels and computers functioned in dual mode English and Arabic. The SBS tech specialist set about reading the manual and spent the voyage on his satellite phone to the UK discussing best options on how to reset the system. Should anyone enter the SBS were ordered not to shoot to kill, unless absolutely no choice, but rather, hold them up and tie them up. The building Jack was in had four guards two at the main gate on the outside and two inside. That was it. Inside he had one man monitoring him 24/7. Thermal imagery from the satellite confirmed this. The former Libyan leader's son, lived in a discreet, more humble part of town compared to what he was used to so as to avoid scrutiny. He had a small entourage of five men accompanying him at any time, all armed. This capture would be risky as his men were ordered to shoot anyone who made an attempt on him. The SAS were given authority to shoot to kill by Mike on this mission. In fact, Mike, didn't care, he wanted the former Leader's son on the aircraft carrier for him to interrogate personally. Mike had the Director of UK Special Forces run through the plan over again. Each time throwing in curve balls like, helicopter engine failure, helicopter shot down, man down, etc. They ran the numbers and the second night the mission was a go. All three missions would take place within hours of each other from midnight, it was a Friday. Jack had been held for two weeks already, his beard had grown, he smelled, he looked like a tramp. His clothes torn. Shoes taken from him. Bruised and battered. He had thankfully not been physically tortured that badly. The night of the operation, all ships and aircraft had their live ammunition loaded into all weapons systems. Mike had ordered that once the mission was complete, that Tomahawk cruise missiles would be launched and destroy the building where Jack was held and the former leader's sons house (which thankfully had no immediate neighbours). The helicopters were all on the flight deck. Four wildcats, four Apache's, they launched on the second mission an hour after the first four speed boats had launched to the radar station. Once launched the next two Merlin helicopters launched with two Apache helicopters as escort to the capture mission. It was an overcrowded flight deck at first. F35B launched, four of them equipped with laser guided bombs, free fall bombs and land attack missiles in the form of Maverick and HARMs, Storm Shadow cruise missiles as well. They had the complete mix for Close Air Support (CAS) should it be needed. The aircraft were ordered to circle Tripoli at 35,000 feet, an RAF Voyager tanker was also tasked to the area for aerial refuelling as required. It was a large-scale operation for the UK Military, the first of its kind coordinated like this for an age. The SBS team reached the radar station without a problem, leaving their boats on the beach. They scaled the rock face without a problem. They were in position to breach station security waiting for the signal, 'Go Go Go', came over loud and clear on the radio. They went in, without a hitch and secured the station, reprogrammed the radar and left discreetly without a sound. The signal went for launch of the carriers airwing as outlined previously, the carrier task group then turned inside Libyan waters at full speed and headed for ten miles off the coast of Tripoli. The Wildcat helicopters approached Jack's building and the SAS fast roped down onto the roof. The Wildcats would take off and the SAS would exit one hundred metres up the road on foot to a field where the Wildcats would eventually pick them up again. It was loud, try to imagine four helicopter engines roaring as they hovered over the building. As they did the guards opened fire, the escorting Apache's opened fire cutting them in half. Once inside the SAS ran downstairs to the basement, the eight men stormed the main hall where Jack's guard was waiting. He opened fire with his AK47. It was a brief fire fight as the SAS threw a stun then a smoke grenade. Rushing the guard and killing him. By now the alert had been raised and the former Leader's son woken. As he was talking on the phone, he heard gun fire outside. The Apache's over head had used their chain guns, but not after the eight man team (all of whom had silenced automatic weapons) on the ground had come under sustained fire and were unable to move from their position. The two guards at the house were killed, two more rushed out only to be shot dead by the SAS as they stormed the house from all sides. There was now only one guard left inside and the son. Both armed. The SAS ordered the Apache to fire using thermal imaging they knew the precise location of the guard. He died immediately. Only the son left. As the SAS approached his room, they had to watch for booby traps, fortunately there were none. The son fired his AK47 and ran out of bullets, the SAS stormed his room, tasering him. They grabbed him by both arms and carried him outside. Where down the road a Merlin helicopter was waiting in the middle of the street, rotors on. The SAS quickly clambered aboard and the Merlin took off rapidly. The escorting Apache's followed suit and the second Merlin with snipers on board, also exited the area. They were ordered to climb rapidly to get out of Surface to Air Missile (SAM) range. By now Jack had been broken out of jail, he was running badly on foot to the Wildcats waiting in the field nearby. The SAS covered Jack and helped him on board the first chopper. The four Apache's whirled overhead as all the SAS were extracted. All helicopters took off and headed back to base. By now the SBS had already nearly reached the taskforce which was about ten miles from the *Rendezvous* point. Fortunately for the British there were no casualties. How lucky they were, but they had the element of surprise on all three missions. As the helicopters approached the carrier, Mike said turn on the landing lights and with that, the entire ships deck lit up. One after another the entire helicopter force landed. The SBS were approaching HMS *Somerset* and extracted from the sea. All ships turned and headed north at flank speed. Heading to Gibraltar. The Four F35 were ordered to return to base and the Voyager also headed to Gibraltar. Jack gingerly got off the helicopter and walked briskly to the entrance of the aircraft carrier hangar stairwell. Where he was greeted by Mike Scott who gave him a hug and said 'are you alright?' Once all personnel were back on board HMS *Queen Elizabeth* and Mike had those SBS on HMS *Somerset* helicopter over too. He held a massive meeting in the main hangar of the ship. There was a huge buzz about the place and all the men were assembled. A huge roar came out from all gathered there when Jack was presented by Mike. Both men were heroes of sorts. Jack waved and said 'thank you' promising to shake everyone's hand in due course.

Jack was doing the rounds thanking all the staff and crew. Everyone was relieved the operation went off without any casualties for the UK. Whilst they all stood round having a drink, they heard the roar of a missile launch. It was the Tomahawks from HMS *Ambush*. Everyone watched on the giant monitor as five missiles were launched, target was the aforementioned buildings. The missiles took ten minutes to hit their targets. Now the only problem was the fact that the UK had launched said missiles without US permission. Much military equipment is sold by the US to other nations, including the UK, on the condition that they ask permission to use it. The UK was about to get told off diplomatically speaking. The good news was that Prime Minister Albrighton didn't care what the US said. Secretly the US was happy. But in public the media fallout had already begun. Someone in the White House leaked the top line details of the mission to the media. The headline ran, 'UK SAS in daring mission to rescue hostage in Libya'. Mike's satellite phone began to ring, it was the PM, asking what happened. Mike explained and the PM was happy. Detail wasn't the PMs strong point. So it wasn't long before the UK Media started asking questions. It was breaking news first thing at seven am in the morning. Reporters buzzed the Defence Secretary and Foreign Secretary respectively. Holding statements were given out, 'we don't comment on special forces operations'. But one journalist said, 'this is half the Royal Navy? And who is Cakebread?' They clamoured to find out more. They found his Twitter feed, they knew instantly that he was a former Director at *UKDO* and they saw the pinned tweet about 'Cakebread' being the codename for Osama Bin Ahmed. They also discovered that Jack had held various other low level political positions over the years. Fortunately for him, a 'D' notice was issued by the MoD saying only positive news stories were acceptable to be published. The UK media were told Jack was just an ordinary citizen in a case of mistaken identity. Later than morning at ten am, a briefing was released live to the assembled media pack. Details of what had happened, how Jack was setup and kidnapped, where he was taken and how he was tortured. The media couldn't understand why so much effort and military hardware was used to rescue him? The MoD admitted that he was former friends of Mike Scott when at *UKDO* and the PM had decided a UK citizen should be rescued given the brazen nature of the kidnapping and torture. Jack Cakebread's face was all over the internet and would be on the front pages of the next day's news. The PM loved positive PR, especially the kind where the UK looked good. The media asked where Jack was, they were told he was *en route* to *Portsmouth* Naval Base. The medical teams felt it best to keep Jack on board the ship and evaluate him as the ship returned to *Portsmouth* Naval Base. Once returned to England, he would be released. On board Jack asked Mike for personal protection officers once in the UK, which was granted along with a full police escort. Mike said the media wanted a press conference, to which Jack said he would gladly give one in Whitehall the following day. It took two days for HMS *Queen Elizabeth* to reach home port. Jack was fine, tucking into the mess hall and generally speaking to as many people as he was allowed. The MI6 officers wanted to debrief him with Mike present to which he agreed. He told them everything that went on and everything he knew. Meanwhile, the former Libyan leader's son was held in the brig on board. His arrest and detention was not made public at first, but yet even that leaked. He on the other hand was sent to Belmarsh prison where he would be put on trial for crimes against humanity and war crimes as a former official in the Libyan government. The aircraft carrier swept slowly into Portsmouth harbour with thousands of people lining the quayside. The flight deck had all the jets and helicopters present and the ships welcomed them in. The Red Arrows did a fly past even, Jack was amazed. Mike Scott told Jack that the PM wanted a big splash for his return and wanted to meet him personally at Downing Street later that day. Jack said, 'I need to go home first and get changed please'. To which Mike said fine take a helicopter and go home first, Jack went home to his mum's house near Biggin Hill. So, it was easy for the Royal Navy helicopter to chopper him home within twenty minutes. Upon arrival a police escort would take him to his mum's house, where he still had a bedroom. His mum was waiting along with the rest of his family and girlfriend. He still had a girlfriend, although she was angry with him for falling for the girls and going to their house to party. Jack denied any sexual relations, which was a blatant lie, but she believed him. She was just happy to see him. Jack and his family were all invited up to Downing Street. Two Mercedes Vito van taxis were arranged, and the police escorted them all the way up to Whitehall, lights flashing all the way. Upon arrival at Downing Street, they entered via the back gate. The media was assembled and what a pack it was. Jack said, he would first do a public interview in the Downing Street media room, then he wanted an exclusive with Nigel Durant of *UK News*. Prime Minister Albrighton waited at the front door of number ten. Jack was ushered through the gates, past the cars and a staffer was briefing Jack on what to expect. A photo op with the PM and then a brief press conference with the PM. Jack couldn't believe he had finally made it politically speaking at least. 'Are you in the SAS' was the first question, 'no', replied Jack. 'Are you a spy', 'no', said Jack. 'Then how are you involved?' 'It is a long story' said Jack. 'A case of mistaken identity. I can't say much more at this stage, however, what I can say is it is better that the Prime Minister take these questions. I am not qualified to answer, Prime Minister, over to you'. The PM smiled, clearly pleased that Jack didn't prattle on or breakdown. The PM, used the media energy to propel himself forward for a local by election coming up the next week. It was politics after all. Once done, Jack was escorted out of the room by the PM to a quieter waiting room where Mike and Jack's family were. Jack took the opportunity to ask the PM whether he would be compensated financially for what went on? The PM looked a little surprised at first and said he would 'get back to him'. Jack said to Mike, 'I want you to be my official liaison please with the government otherwise I will get nothing. Anything I do get, I will give you Mike Scott, ten percent'. Mike ever the businessman, agreed. 'What are you after said Mike?' 'A hundred million pounds please. I think that is fair after what I have been put through the past ten years, let alone the past couple of weeks'. Mike said, 'leave it with me'. Before Mike could leave, Jack said, to him, 'I'd like an answer before I leave tonight, please'. 'Ok' said Mike. Jack told his family that he was waiting for some updates before he would leave, Jack's family had been told the private reception would end at ten pm sharp. Jack had a couple of hours spare. Mike on the other hand walked out and found the Prime Minister's office. He knocked on the door and said 'one small matter to discuss Harry. Compensation for Cakebread. He wants two hundred million pounds'. 'He wants what?!' Said the PM. 'No chance, far too much'. 'Think of the goodwill Harry, Jack will get you re-elected and you'll blow Labour out of the water next week at the by election'. 'Ok' said the PM, but let's first see where we are financially. I will come back to you shortly'. Mike couldn't quite believe it, but he knew the PM well and he knew that the PM trusted him infinitely. Five minutes went by and Mike heard Harry call him back into his office once more. 'You've got the money' said the PM. 'Two hundred million is Cakebread's'. Mike deliberately asked for more, because he felt Jack deserved it. The Treasury Chief was called in and ordered to produce a cheque for Jack Cakebread to the tune of two hundred million pounds. The PM was photographed handing him the cheque. Jack didn't overreact, rather was quietly content with the sum. Mike turned to him later on that evening and said, 'you do know the Chinese were the ones who tipped us off as to your whereabouts. Without them, you'd still be in that dungeon. So don't forget to thank them if you ever get the opportunity'. 'I will' said Jack. With that, the night came to a close and Jack and his family went home to his sisters house in Chelsea to celebrate. Jack gave his family members ten million each including his girlfriend. He kept the rest. Jack would that week go on UK News with Nigel Durant and tell his story as best he could. It drew in ten million viewers, breaking the station record, in fact nearly breaking many records. Now Jack was famous and rich, former girlfriends and women he knew all wanted a piece of him. Most were positive and friendly when the media interviewed them about Jack, however, one was really bitchy, saying she wanted compensation from Jack for allegedly harassing her. Jack said, 'she used to love me at school, now she's upset. She missed her opportunity I'm afraid' and that was all he had to say. Jack would later become a donor to the Conservative Party and a philanthropist in a limited capacity. He would eventually leave London to move to Switzerland. Keeping a flat in London, Vienna, Munich, Dubai and Geneva. Mike Scott on the other hand retired to St Lucia in the Caribbean. Harry Albrighton went on to win the next election. And China became number one worldwide, still monitoring Jack for his own good, in case the Libyans ever came back.

The End.

Printed in Great Britain
by Amazon

20170087R00051